DEEP BLUE

J. Turbett

For Jake

Table of Contents

Prologue

Looking back, I'm not really sure I could describe how things got so entirely out of hand. They say when writing a story you should start from the beginning, there's so much to say, and it seems so hard to understand that I guess the beginning is as good a place to start as any. I have a story to tell and I will tell it my way or no way at all. I didn't go from being some average kid to the leader of a nation in a fortnight, you know. Someone has to destroy the misconceptions about us, and as much as I hate to admit it, the only person qualified to tell the tale is me.

My mate tells me I need to accept the hand that's dealt to me, and I work so hard every day. I have to say this isn't a responsibility I ever wanted, and after everything that has happened, I've lost more than I can say in one paragraph. What I've gained is a wonderland of knowledge and beauty, an environment no human can ever contemplate knowing, and the love of my life. Whether it was all worth it, perhaps someone will tell me someday.

So, here we are, together, at the beginning. Our story begins as many do, with a girl: a girl lost to misfortune and tragedy. She'd all but given up on her life and her family, but her family didn't want to give up on her. They decided to move to a small town on the relatively unpopulated western shore of Australia, a place called Brassila Cove. A place more than touched by the ocean, and if there's one thing I can tell you, the ocean is big...

Chapter 1

The Ocean

Adam Carson sat at his desk, looking through his clinic's tiny window to the sun glinting off the ocean. It was late July, and he was expecting the Bailey family to come in today. They were from the states, someone had told him, and he was to be their guide. It was only appropriate, considering it was his old house they had purchased. He was loath to leave the little house, but he needed to be closer to the ocean. If someone described his old place as a "three-bedroom house," they would be exaggerating; the other two bedrooms were actually more like large closets. Unfortunately, the realtor had reminded him that the house was virtually unsellable without a bit of work, so repairmen were currently crawling all over it. He sighed, took a sip of coffee and started gathering his things.

"I'm off to meet the newcomers, Natalie," he said to his assistant as he toted his briefcase out into the waiting room.

"Good luck," she mumbled. It was no secret that newcomers weren't generally welcome in Brassila Cove. Then again, Ronald Bailey seemed perfectly friendly on the phone.

The town of Brassila Cove was built onto a stepped incline, as if it had been carved from a cliff-face. The storms were brutal, but the town managed to weather almost everything. People came and went as often as the seasons but there was a small core that made the town their permanent berth.

He knew the Baileys would be arriving at the resort soon. It was a fair walk from his office to the highest point where the resort sat, but he looked forward to it. The sun shone on his face as he passed everyone he knew. He waved at the small town baker, side-stepped the truck driving at half-a-mile an hour carrying fish for the fish-market. Before he knew it he was climbing the last bit of the way and coming upon the little hotel they lovingly called the resort.

The resort was small; there weren't a high number of tourists that came to Brassila Cove. Those who did were often just looking for a break from city life. Brassila Cove was a closely guarded secret, a local phenomenon. He looked down toward the ocean, down at the Caraway mansion. The mansion was about five times larger than the resort. He smiled to himself. This little town protected a secret so much larger than most would ever know.

A secret as large as the ocean itself, and a history that spanned into folklore.

Chapter 2

The Baileys

The Jeep hit a bump and Alice was jarred awake. Her forehead was red where it had pressed against the window. She blinked at the sunlight, and saw nothing but barren land. Slowly, the sounds of the world came back to her: the rumbling of the Jeep's engine, the noises of her teenage brother's DS as he played beside her. She looked over at him, intent in his game, just as oblivious to their surroundings as she was. Their parents sat in the front; they seemed to be the only people happy about this move.

Sarah and Ronald were typical good parents. Ronald was tall and gangly, with glasses and wild, honey-colored hair. His wife, Sarah, was short and sweet. Her wavy brown hair was cropped short. David had his mother's brown hair and freckles; he was gangly in the way only a 17-year-old can be. Alice was something else: Alice looked like a corpse. Her long hair was dark, tangled and unkempt; it hung flat against her and hid everything it could. What her hair didn't hide, her baggy clothes did. Her eyes were sunk into her skull as if they were hiding from something, the dark circles under her eyes describing just how little sleep Alice ever found. Though she was seven years older than David, he could have picked her up with one arm.

Alice finally forced her eyes to focus on the world around her as they burst into the town. Ronald slowed the Jeep, avoiding pedestrians as they crossed the street. The pedestrians watched them curiously; there wasn't much welcome to be found there. Alice didn't really care to find the eyes of anyone, and she would prefer if no one found hers either.

"We're almost there!" Ronald said excitedly as Sarah smiled at him and gripped his hand. Alice stared out the window.

"Brassila Cove," her mother said mistily.

"Great. How tiny is this place, anyway?" David asked.

"About 5,000," Ron replied, "Nice and quiet,"

"Completely cut off from the main city," Sarah said.

"Self-contained."

"Beautiful."

"Perfect for a botanist."

"Or a dentist."

Ron and Sarah smiled at each other.

David rolled his eyes. "Well, at least someone's happy we're out in the middle of nowhere," he muttered.

Ronald frowned, glancing into the rear-view mirror at his son, whose gaze remained fixed on his video game. "This is a great opportunity for us young man. We all decided this was the right move,"

"I changed my mind," David mumbled, "Australia was supposed to be cool. So far it's just boring." His parents didn't even dignify this newest protest with a response.

Alice ignored the conversation inside the car and watched the city. Though they were obviously indifferent to outsiders, people seemed happy here. Maybe it was the sun, clearly more common here than back home in Portland, Oregon. The sky there was always gray, but Alice didn't miss it. Alice didn't miss anything. She noticed glimpses of the ocean flicker between houses and businesses. It was beautiful, but all Alice saw was gray. She reached through a haze of nothingness and so little touched her.

Ronald pulled into the parking lot of the Brassila Resort. An overgrown hotel, the place was small, maybe fifty rooms. It was decorated Tiki-style, heavy on the bamboo. A worn sign announced that the pool was closed for the season, and it had clearly been dry for some time. The place had charm but it was definitely a somewhat decayed charm.

"Well, grab your stuff, kids: we're here!" Ron announced. The two parents jumped out of their seats while David grudgingly put away his electronics. Alice slowly opened the door and stepped to the ground without excitement or argument. Sarah stole a glance at her daughter. They were used to her demeanor by now. After the tragedy she had suffered some of it was understandable. On the other hand it had been so long and she still hadn't even begun to recover. They hoped being close to a tropical ocean, in a town with little to no crime, where everyone knew who everyone was, would do her good. Something that they couldn't do for her.

"I hope we're doing the right thing," Sarah whispered to her husband.

"Me, too. I just wish we could have the old Aly back," Ron said.

"Maybe she'll start swimming again!"

"Don't get your hopes up too much, dear." They watched her follow slowly behind them as David tugged at a large suitcase in the back of the Jeep.

They checked in at the desk, a giant fake palm shading them as they signed the ledger. The pimple-faced desk clerk gave them a key and pointed up the staircase. He looked bored, like he'd do anything to get out of the little town.

"What? No elevator?" David yelped. The attendant just shook his head. David glanced down at his luggage. Mostly electronics, it wasn't exactly light, and he looked up at his mom in horror.

"Come on, honey, it'll be good for you," she smiled, patting him on the shoulder. They made a procession up the stairs, Sarah and Ronald in front, Alice still quietly following behind, and David bringing up the rear, breathing heavily and cursing his parents for bringing him to this stupid town.

"Oh, look at this place!" Her mother yelped when they made it to the room. Alice glanced apathetically out the window. It was open to the outside, and there was a view of the ocean and a gorgeous mansion down on the beach. She had heard her parents discussing it: some millionaire or something owned it and the surrounding beach.

She turned back toward the room. The two double beds and chairs were made of a worn wicker; the desk was a brown wood that looked like it had been cooked by the sun. Light blue curtains swung in the breeze leading out to a balcony. Alice floated toward that balcony and stared down at the town. There wasn't really any privacy in the room, but Alice had no trouble finding that slow solitude she was accustomed to in her mind. Shut out the sounds, shut out the smells, shut out the light, breathe.

Both parents were fawning over all the quaint details, the local paintings on the walls and the bars of soap in the bathroom, dancing with excitement. They hadn't expected Alice to open up right away, but the apathy of both kids was still mildly disheartening.

David was busy opening his suitcase and setting up his laptop on the rickety desk, the chair squeaking noisily. Abruptly, David huffed with frustration.

"Mom! There's no internet in this place. What kind of a hotel doesn't have internet?"

"I think you can survive without internet for a few days,

David," Sarah sighed, in a way only a mother could. David glared at her, then booted up a game.

Suddenly, there was a knock at the door. Opening it, Ronald said, "Hi! You must be Dr. Carson."

"And you must be Dr. Bailey," the young doctor responded as he stepped into the room. "You can call me Adam." He had deep brown eyes and dark, dark hair. He moved with an innate confidence, as if he owned the town.

Sarah moved forward quickly and grabbed his hand, shaking it vigorously. "I'm Ron's wife, Sarah, and these are our children: David, on the computer, and Alice, by the window." Sarah glanced at Alice, curious about her response to the handsome stranger who would be showing them around the town. Alice didn't seem to care; she was just doing her thing where she shut out the world again. Sarah sighed.

Adam nodded at the kids, then turned back to Ronald and Sarah. "I'm sorry that the house isn't quite ready for you yet. They are still working on the roof, and I think the air conditioner has been delayed again. Hopefully by the end of this week."

"Absolutely fine, this place is wonderful," Ronald said.

"Well, can I show you around town? You can even see where your dental practice has been set up, Ronald."

"Oh that would be splendid!" Ronald practically skipped to join the doctor. Neither child moved.

"I think the kids and I will hang back this time," Sarah said. "Adam, where would be a good place for food nearby?"

"There's a diner a couple blocks down. Emelie makes a great fish and chips," Adam mentioned. "Sure you don't want to join us for the tour?"

Sarah shook her head. "I think the kids and I need to get some food in us before we explore much more," she remarked, "But you could walk us to Emelie's!"

After dropping the rest of the family off, Adam walked with Ronald. Mr. Bailey's office wasn't too far from his own. He was looking forward to the new practice: they had never had a dentist in the town before.

"When did you graduate from med school?" Ron asked, looking at Adam puzzled by his youth.

'   "A few years back, with honors." Adam said. He was used to strangers giving him odd looks for his youth.

"Your father must be so proud." Ron said.

"He is. He was excited to move to the city when I came back to take over the local clinic here."

"He was a doctor, too?"

"Yeah, runs in the family, I guess. How about your kids?" Adam asked. Ronald frowned in response.

"Well a couple years back my Aly had," he paused, "some

14

problems." Adam eyed him but didn't press, and Ronald continued hesitantly. "Her and her brother used to be real close. When Aly got distant, Davy buried himself in his games and computers." Ronald sighed. "Alice ended up dropping out of college. Here's a picture of her a few years ago." Ron pulled a photo from his wallet. It was Alice's senior picture from high school. In it, her hair, the same pale color as her father's but with her mother's waves, was cut a little below her shoulders. Her green eyes shone at the camera and she had a smile that could break your heart.

"She's beautiful." Adam said.

"She was," Ron frowned, "Her mother and I were hoping maybe the sun and the small town would do her good, bring her back."

"What made you decide on Brassila Cove?"

"Well, Sarah got an opportunity at the school up in the city, and then, I dunno; something about this little town just jumped off the page for us."

"Well whatever the reason," Adam said, stepping aside to open the door to Ronald's new office, "I'm glad you're here."

Sarah, David, and Alice headed out to the diner. David was keeping pace but dragging his feet, and Alice, as always was behind. She bumped into a passing young woman.

"Watch where you're going, retard!" the girl snapped. Alice

looked up. The stranger was about Alice's age and looked way too fashionable for this area. Her bright bikini top perfectly complimented the highlights in her brown hair and brown eyes. Alice mumbled an apology, perplexed at her manner. Though others in the town had been cold, no one else seemed so easily offended.

The girl was already rushing past, headed down toward the beach. Sarah and David had already disappeared behind the doors of the diner, and Alice followed them, then almost walked straight back out as the first strains of "Mr. Sandman" began to play. David was stock still, looking like he was about to throw up. Their mother clapped her hands in delight. Alice was just stunned. The whole diner was so strange that even she came out of the clouds for a moment. She stared around and wondered if she had walked into a time warp. If nothing else had said they weren't in Portland anymore that diner would have said it all.

Her mother slid into one of the red vinyl booths. David followed, looking green. While David stared at the table, Sarah and her daughter looked around at the locals. They looked fairly average, a couple of fishers, a small family with a young baby in the corner, a couple surfers. One guy at the counter was surrounded by three girls, all four as fashionable as the girl who had bumped into Alice outside.

The guy was wearing a collared shirt, strategically unbuttoned, his chest and washboard abs clearly visible. He had a swimmer's bod on a lean frame, and was probably at least six foot. His sun-bleached hair and strong cheekbones framed a perpetually annoyed look. He reminded Alice vaguely of Spike from Buffy the Vampire Slayer, only younger. She had watched so many of those episodes with her roommate from college, who had owned all the seasons. Shaking her head, Alice wiped away thoughts of her old life as fast as she could; she didn't want to remember college, or her roommate for that matter.

Sarah was watching the strange young man as well; a blush crept to her cheeks though she was at least twice his age. She could understand the women around him. He turned, feeling a gaze upon him, and shot her an irritated look. In Sarah's eyes it looked like he just wanted to get away from the women, from the diner. She turned back to her children as she heard the waitress approach, and they ordered a few of the specials. As the waitress walked away, Sarah glanced around the diner again.

"Isn't this place cute?" she asked. Alice didn't respond, sinking back into her clouds.

"This is a nightmare!" David said. The two began bickering, then arguing. David always in his computer and fake worlds, for Sarah he felt as distant as her daughter. Sarah and Ronald hadn't yet given up on Alice; at least they knew what she had been through. They still couldn't imagine what it was like for Alice, they couldn't imagine how completely it had destroyed her. Alice just sank further and further away every time they tried to help. Alice lived far from the world of reality. Maybe even farther than her brother. Sarah hated arguing with David, but at least they were talking to each other.

"They don't even have internet in the hotel!" David whined.

"We'll have internet when we get to our home."

"We won't be there for another week!"

"Just relax and enjoy the scenery, honey. You could even explore the town, do something outside for a change!" Sarah tried to keep the exasperation out of her voice but failed.

"I'll do something outside when she does," David pouted, nodding toward Alice with his arms folded across his chest. He stared across the table at his sister, but she was just staring into space. It was a long moment before she even realized she was being stared at, and then she turned her face away again.

"One Beef and Reef and two fish and chips." The waitress' interruption halted David's musings, and stopped his mother from going into convulsions of frustration.

"Why, thank you," Sarah looked up at the waitress, forcing her most winning smile. One child dead to the world, the other one angry at being left behind. It was more than a mother was ever meant to handle.

David huffed, forcing himself to stare at his own food. He couldn't take it, watching his sister poke at yet another meal without really eating it. She could have almost passed for a skeleton already. The transformation had happened right before his eyes, and the shell sitting across the table wasn't his sister at all. It was the muscle mass she had lost first, then her hair had grown to cover her face, and she became further and further from anyone's reach, even his.

Alice stared out the window at the calmingly provincial scene. She saw people milling about, the blond guy leaving the diner, followed by his harem, forcing people to make way on either side. It didn't matter; when she closed her eyes, all she saw was the darkness, all she heard was the gasping, all she smelled was blood. The world around her was nothing but a gnat flying around her face. There was another smell, fighting for dominance over the scent of blood she never forgot: the ocean, the deep blue environment she could almost surrender to, but she wouldn't. She didn't want to wake up, she didn't want to be a part of this world, a world where all bright things turned dark eventually. At the same time, she could see herself on the diving board, feel the water as she sped through it at competition, she could hear the cheers of the audience, none louder than her brother. She had to shut it off, she had no choice, the next time she found comfort someone would challenge it again, she was powerless as a slug against the salt, and worthless. Shut out the sounds, shut out the smells, shut out the light, breathe. It was the only way she could retain a shred of sanity. The only way she could hold her broken pieces together.

Ronald watched his wife bring the steaming cup of tea to her lips. Sarah was wrapped in a blanket in a wicker chair on the porch. Inside, Alice was asleep facing a wall; if he didn't know she was asleep, he could have believed her dead. David slept on the couch, arms crossed across his chest as if he were still angry, even in sleep. Ronald shivered at the breeze coming off the ocean. The way Sarah looked over the water reminded him eerily of the way Alice stared at everything; empty. He walked over to her and laid his hand on her shoulder, wanting to interrupt that look in the worst way. He didn't need to lose his wife too.

She looked up at him with her endearing smile on her face, but there was loss there too, and worry. He took the seat across from her. "What is it?" he whispered, keeping his voice low.

"What is it always, honey?"

"I thought we agreed we wouldn't send her to the hospital." He said casting an askew glance to the door and the sleeping kids inside.

Sarah looked at him pleadingly. "You should have seen her at the diner today. She's no better. It's like she only gets worse. If only she would just talk to me, help me understand."

"We've been down this road," he took her free hand, and squeezed it, trying to encourage his shaken wife.

"I thought the smell of the ocean would bring her back to us, but all it truly did was drive her further from us. David is right:

20

why should he participate in this world when his sister is the walking dead?"

"It's too soon to say that this move isn't helping. We have to have faith in her."

"We've put so much faith in her already! We've moved her several places, we've uprooted her life and now we've crossed the ocean, all in the hopes of getting her to smile again." She looked up at her husband, her big chestnut brown eyes glimmering with tears. Ronald took a deep breath and looked out over the sea. Sarah was right: they were near their wit's end with their daughter. Since she had returned from California she hadn't participated in anything, she refused to be present for any event, and this was the last straw. They couldn't undo the move, there had been so much tragedy for Alice there, and the loss of Ron's mother affected him more than he would dare show the kids, so a new start was needed for them all, but if this didn't work, he didn't know what should come next.

"We have to give her a couple of months; let the sunshine and the new environment do their work," he sighed, "If things don't improve we'll send her to a hospital."

Sarah contemplated her husband. He was so worn down by this, more than she had let herself realize. She could swear there were a few more wrinkles in his familiar face. He spoke the truth though: they had been in Australia all of two days.

Inside on the couch, David didn't move and made sure his

21

breathing was regular, but he heard every word. It wasn't like he hadn't heard them discussing sending her to the hospital before. It wouldn't change anything, anyway. If she went to the hospital it would just mean that no one would have to look at the shell of the person she used to be. At the same time, he felt a wet tear roll down his cheek. It used to be them against the world, him and Alice. When the big kids picked on him and his freckles in school, it was she who was there for him.

He'd tried to be there for her this time, but she wasn't there. His parents' faith was unfounded, and as he fell back into his troubled sleep he wondered how long it would take Alice to find the local bar.

Chapter 3

Brassila Cove

It took Alice a week to find the local bar and grill, much longer than David had anticipated. He was sitting across from her in the middle of the new living room, watching her mechanically opening boxes and looking inside until she found the one from her bedroom. She opened the box, then stared at it for several minutes before getting up and leaving the house. His parents thought she'd go to the sea or something, but David knew: his parents didn't keep alcohol in the house anymore, so Alice had to find the bar.

As the door slammed shut behind her, David got up and went to the box Alice had opened. He picked up the item on top, amidst a pile of ribbons and trophy's, the picture frame. Tabitha was there, and so was Tabby's brother, and David, everyone smiling. Alice had just won the gold at a swim meet and was posing in front with her medal, meat on her bones and that ingratiating smile on her face. David threw the frame back in the box with a clatter.

"David, are you all right?" Sarah shouted over the racket of dishes being unpacked and put away.

"I'm fine, mom." David picked up Alice's box of knickknacks and shoved it away at the bottom of the tiny linen closet.

"Isn't that from Alice's room?" his mother asked, coming up behind him.

He rounded on her angrily. "Who's Alice?!" he stomped up the stairs before she could stop him and slammed his door shut. He didn't need to listen to her shouts of outrage.

Every small town has its bar. To Alice's credit, her family had been very busy that day. The truck with their stuff had arrived before the house was ready, and so they had stored everything at the resort. Then, when the house was ready, they had to move the boxes from the resort to their small little house, one Jeep-full at a time. It had been late afternoon before the family had been able to do any unpacking, and Ron was already at work.

The bar she had found wasn't far up from the ocean. The front was unremarkable; it was a mock-up of a plank leading to a boat. Inside it was worn wood the color of coconut, with a tropical theme similar to the resort. It almost made Alice sick to look at it. There was a loft with extra seating that led to a balcony. It could almost have been a repurposed warehouse but Alice didn't really see a purpose for there being a warehouse in such a small town. The back of the building was lined with windows that looked over the ocean and made the bar seem far more open than it should. Bars were supposed to be closed in, intimate and dark. The only time this bar was dark was when the sun set.

There was a door in the back that led to a yard where tables sat unevenly on the ground creating even more seating that the bar didn't really need, however most of the tables and chairs were pushed to the side to accommodate the band. The band was playing soft reggae music that night. It fit with the cheesy décor very well. The backyard ended in a sheer cliff with only a half-wall made of bricks to keep you from falling over; it could double as seating or a place to put your drinks, but there had to be some safety violations. Then again who would care about the safety violations at a small bar in the middle of Nowhere, Australia? It seemed that the idea here was that if you were dumb enough to fall over the wall, then you deserved it. What Alice liked was that the smells of the grill and the booze nearly overpowered the intoxicating smell of the ocean.

Alice loved the smell of the ocean. She wouldn't go down to it but it was as much of a drug as the alcohol she was pouring into herself that night. She was already going crazy with nothing to do in this town. That smell, the smell of the ocean, dredged up memories she had avoided for so long. The bartender could see that the new girl was probably going to be a regular: she looked like she was carrying the weight of the world on her shoulders.

He nodded at the doctor when Adam entered through the giant plastic coconut doorway. Adam noticed Alice immediately, and smiled a little. She looked so far gone, but he couldn't resist. He walked up to the bar. Adam had always kind of had a thing for lost causes, even in medical school. The truth was someone had to. If you always wrote off a lost cause, none of them would get saved. Sometimes you even got lucky when you poured your best effort into one. So this night he approached her as he would any patient who didn't have a chance in the world, with a friendly smile, all his attention focused on her waning vital signs.

"Aren't you a little young to be drinking?" She looked up.

"Aren't you a little young to be a doctor?"

"So you do speak!" the doctor retorted, ordering a drink. *Great, a comedian,* Alice thought, but his joke hit close to home: the only time she ever did speak was when drinking. She hoped that he would lose interest and be on his way soon. At the same time, she had a good buzz going, and he was looking at her expectantly as he leaned against the bar.

"I'm twenty-three," she said, resigning herself to conversation.

"Well, I'm twenty-eight," Adam replied, noticing the dilated pupils of her eyes, and the faint glow on her cheeks.

"Wonderful." Alice got up to go. It wasn't that the doctor wasn't attractive. It was just Alice didn't trust men, especially when they had a drink or two in them. She would never make that mistake again.

"How do you like the town so far?" Adam asked, turning to face her, not put off at all. Alice turned to him and sighed, he wasn't going to go away, and he was ruining her buzz.

"It's okay." She answered, settling back onto the stool and putting her escape plans on hold for the moment.

"Your father told me you used to be quite the swimmer."

"Used to." She didn't move to continue the conversation. That would deter most people but it seemed that Adam was more difficult to get rid of.

"Come on, let's find a table. I'll buy you a drink." Alice hesitated. She didn't have to talk to him, but if he was offering to buy her a drink. Her funds *were* getting low pretty quick. She turned and walked to the back of the room, settling into an empty booth. It was as much of an invitation as she was likely to give, so Adam followed.

"Have you met any interesting people?" he asked as they sat down.

"Where's the drink you offered me?"

Adam cringed a little but got them a pitcher anyway.

"Well?" he asked when the waiter had come and gone.

"You may not have realized this, but I like to keep to myself," she answered rudely.

He smiled at her. It was a winning smile, would turn the inside of most women to mush, but Alice was made of stone. She stared back at him emptily in response to it. She certainly wasn't making this easy for him.

"You're in a new country now, in a tiny town; there's got to be something you've noticed here." She was silent almost to the point of him breaking, it sent shivers down his spine. He was nearly ready to give up when she finally spoke.

"The beach: so private you'll get shot for trespassing?" From her Dad's office, she could see signs guarding the beach adjacent to the mansion. In a small town it seemed strange to her that someone would use deadly force to protect their property. Adam stared back at her, considering her over his beer. On the one hand, he had the girl talking; on the other hand, the Caraway family wasn't really a topic he liked bringing up. She was new to the town, though, and he did have her talking.

One of the guitarists from the band outside had started coming around to the tables, playing a sweet reggae ballad to each table. When he approached Alice she turned to him aggressively. "Fuck off, man." Startled, the guitarist continued to the next table. Alice began to stir, and Adam knew he was about to lose her.

"They're very serious about their privacy, the Caraways are."

Alice turned back to the man. He was looking at her so expectantly there was a part of her that wanted to leap out of the seat and run. She downed the rest of her beer, then took the pitcher to refill it. Adam reached for it at the same time. "Allow me." As his hand brushed hers, she yanked it back as if she had been burned. She stared at him angrily.

"Fuck this. I'm leaving." She moved to stand and leave, wobbling a little on her legs. "I mean, some rich yuppie family has as much business being here as I do, and probably about as much sense to be willing to ask for their own privacy."

Adam stood. There were a couple of eyes on them, townsfolk who were familiar to Adam but still strangers to Alice. "Please," Adam started, "I'm sorry if I offended you in some way. Please don't go." He trailed off, she turned to look at him, and for an instant his brown eyes met her green eyes ones. Inside them he saw not anger but fear, and he knew, he knew at least part of what Alice hid from. Sometimes it was hard working with humans, and she was so tragically hurt in a way he certainly wasn't trained in fixing. She wasn't moving, she was staring at him staying as far from him as possible, his touch made her almost ill. Quickly he filled her mug of beer and sat back down. "You're right, they don't really have a right to ask for privacy, but they have the money and they have the firepower, too. This is *their* town."

The way he said the town was theirs made her wonder. Carefully she sidled back into her seat. She was sitting as far away from him as she could. He knew he had slipped up a little, the shadowed girl was much more perceptive than he realized and he knew he would have to pick his words carefully in her presence. "You must have seen one of the Caraways. I've heard the eldest is back in town for the moment," he said, carefully drawing his arm away from the mug, slowly so as not to spook her. She watched him carefully before reaching out to pull the mug back to herself.

"I don't really care to know anyone here," she said pointedly, under her breath as she began pouring the poison down her throat again. Adam was beginning to understand the plight of the Bailey parents.

"Well no one really cares to know Finn Caraway. Especially after they do take the time to get to know him." She narrowed her eyes as she looked at him, as if she was going to pull a gun on him if he kept talking. He stopped just for the moment, watching her drink her beer. She was truly trying to drown herself in the depths of the pitcher. He looked at her, the pallor of her skin, the oil in her hair, the air of discontent. She didn't want to be a part of reality, and he was making it worse on her. Perhaps he was drinking too much himself. He sighed softly; she didn't even notice.

"There's an old legend about the town," he said, hoping to engage her with a fairy tale. She peered through her unkempt hair suspiciously. Adam smiled, a weak smile, but a hopeful one all the same.

"You're good at manipulating people, aren't you?" she said as he ordered her another drink from the wandering barmaid.

"You just look like you want your mind off things, anything I can do to help..." he let it hang. She didn't answer so he continued. "So, once upon a time," she raised her eyebrows, "That's how stories are supposed to start right?" he grinned.

"Whatever."

"Anyway, there was this man named Matthew Caraway. He was a millionaire of some sort. Old money, I think, some kind of British blue blood. He loved the country and would go out in the bush in search of adventure, as most yuppies were wont to do." He took a breath, watching her, "He was the type who was never happy in one place, and everyone knew he would probably die young, taking his money with him, because there wasn't a single woman who could catch his eye." She wasn't looking at him, so he couldn't tell if she was listening or not, but she wasn't leaving and that's what mattered.

"Until, one night, that all changed. On a beach somewhere he met a woman. Her hair was long, as if it had never been cut, and her body was like no woman's he had ever seen. She danced with him for one night while he made camp on that beach. Her name was Brassila." Alice's eyebrows raised, it was the only indication he had that she was hearing him.

"The next morning when he woke, it was if she had never existed, except for a hairnet he found woven of sea grass and pearls. He was mad with love for the woman, and he found something new to hunt. He chased her all across the continent, all along the coastline. He followed rumors of the long-haired beauty. He couldn't find her anywhere, but he refused to give up the search." Alice was looking at him now, listening.

"Seven years after his first encounter he accidentally ended here. He was far from civilization, half-starved, and ready to give up on life if he couldn't find his mystery woman." He paused for effect but Alice only returned to her drink.

"On that night, under a full moon, she appeared to him again. She poured fresh water on his parched lips and she lay with him again. The next morning he awoke to find himself under shelter, with a large plate of food, and a map that would lead him back to civilization as he knew it. He had thought her a dream again but this time he had absolute proof. The hairnet that he always carried with him was gone."

"He screamed at the sea then, crying for her to return. If she dared keep him alive, than she should also give him her love. He didn't want to live life without her. He screamed until he was exhausted and then made up his mind. He would never leave that shore again. So he spent his entire fortune building his mansion here, and the town sprung up around it. In the '50s this place was really popular with tourists hoping to find the mysterious woman who stole the eligible bachelor's heart away. Or perhaps trying to win the bachelor's heart for themselves, but he never took another woman into his bed."

Alice had finished yet another drink but this time she made no move to refill it, she was waiting, waiting for the end of his story. He didn't dare let himself smile.

"As Matthew Caraway lie on his deathbed in the mansion, a young woman appeared from out of the blue. The girl walked in, and Matthew lay his fading eyes upon her. She walked to his bed, and took his hand. He looked at her and smiled. She wore a tattered dress, and a hairnet, made from sea grass and pearls. His dying wish was that the mansion and the town would pass to this young mystery woman. He died shortly thereafter. Cara took his last name, and many believed her to be Matthew's illegitimate daughter from the only woman he ever loved. Cara passed away and her sons, Finn and Tom, are the caretakers of the mansion now, and the technical owners of the town, although no one has seen Tom in years. Finn comes back every so often."

"What happened to his daughter? To Cara?"

"When Finn was young, starting his career, in music and modeling, his mother died in a tragic boating accident. The town was heartbroken. A nanny showed up from out of town and took care of Finn and his brother as long as they needed it. The town hasn't been the same since."

"Cara sounds like an important lady."

The doctor nodded, "Her and her husband both,"

"What happened to her husband?"

"After Cara's accident he disappeared. No one's seen him since."

Alice sat silent staring at the handsome doctor. She felt the press of night and the ocean breeze around her. She shivered; it was just a stupid fairy-tale but part of it rang true. Of course, those made the best stories, the ones that wound their lies around the truth.

"Do people show up out of nowhere, then disappear often around here?" He laughed. It was a friendly laugh, but it startled her all the same.

"Maybe so often we've become used to it." He said, still chuckling. The laughter made Alice uneasy. He looked at her, contemplating her. She was quite drunk. He held out his white coat, "You look cold."

She stared at it, as if it might attack her, but the breeze running through her hair was chilly. She took it carefully, avoiding his touch; he let her have it easily, not wanting to frighten her. She threw the coat carefully over her shoulders.

"Come on, I'll walk you home." Alice eyed him suspiciously, but she accepted. They walked in silence, her keeping enough distance from him as she could. Nothing disturbed them but the sounds of the ocean far below. He walked her to the little cottage he used to own. It was a sweet little house nestled in between two very large bushes, making the house seem almost as small as a toy. She left him at the gate and walked up the small crumbling path. He watched her back for a moment before turning to leave. He didn't want anything from the girl; he was simply glad had puzzled out a little of her mystery.

Alice didn't stop walking, she didn't stop staring at the ground but as she put her foot on the first step of the creaking stairs she stopped, waiting for the world to stop spinning around her. "Thank you," she mumbled.

Adam's head whipped around in response to the thanks he barely heard. She was disappearing into the house already, but he knew he heard her right. Maybe the girl wasn't as far gone as her parents thought she was. Maybe he had a chance of helping the family. If the others in the town could just give him a quiet season, he might be able to help someone really in need.

Everyone else was asleep when Alice stumbled over boxes still unpacked, and up into her cramped little room, the only thing clear being the single bed pressed against the wall that she quickly fell into. She slipped into her drunken dreamless sleep still in her clothes, and Adam's white coat.

Chapter 4

A Little Swim

It was dark, it was wet, and Alice was freezing. She could smell it, she could smell the blood, she could feel the emptiness inside her. There were monsters here, in the dark and the cold. Every muscle in her body ached, she crawled to her feet and felt the wet between her thighs. She couldn't see it but she knew there was blood there. There he was, the monster with the knife in his hand. He slashed at her and she ran, but she couldn't get away. She was back on the ground, back in the filth and the wet, she couldn't get up, she tried to scream but no sound came from her mouth, and her grandmother stared at her with those empty, empty eyes.

Alice opened her eyes. The empty eyes of the dream were her own. It was a dream she was so familiar with, she didn't cry anymore, she didn't do anything but mechanically crawl from bed, and reach for her clothes. She pulled them on and walked downstairs where David was waiting.

"Mom, I'm 17! I'm not a child anymore!"

Sarah sighed as she cleaned the dishes from the table; she didn't even look at Alice as she entered the room. The plans were in the works. Ron was looking for the right place, but the decision was made: they would send Alice away to a hospital. Neither parent was happy about it, and David least of all. He had figured it out. He stared at his sister with pity. He didn't know what to do. He couldn't bring her out of her darkness anymore than anyone else could.

"Let's go." Alice mumbled, grabbing her purse. David grudgingly obliged. Alice walked David to school as she had for the past week. The school was small and David hated it. He hadn't made a single friend, and having his despondent sister walk him to school every morning didn't help much. Other kids laughed at him. He didn't have anything in common with anyone: they spent their days off barbequing, running, surfing, and doing other sports, while David spent his days off on his computer in the air conditioning.

David knew that, even when Alice was gone, he would be stuck in this town, and he resented her for it. He wanted to slap her, to make her realize they were going to send her away, but it wouldn't have made a difference. He missed their larger house in Portland. Even his grandma's house in L.A. would have been better, even though it always smelled funny. Anywhere was better than Brassila Cove. The people here were Neanderthals to David. The most exciting part of their days was probably going out with BB guns and shooting cats.

A month in this town, and the only thing interesting that had happened was Alice had gone out looking for a job. Granted, she spent all her money at the bar after getting her first paycheck, but it was mildly encouraging for two days. Being out in the sun hadn't changed her, though, and working at the small surf shop where she saw people every day didn't help, either.

Ronald had wondered if he had gone too far when he offered half-off dental work to anyone who would employ his daughter. Ted Grand had taken him up on the offer and Alice had started part-time at the local surf shop. They sold bathing suits and surf boards, and even offered surfing and sailing lessons. It didn't matter anymore. Alice was the same person that her parents didn't recognize. Every day, Alice woke up, got dressed, walked with her brother to school as she used to in the old days, went to work, then went to the bar. The worst was the weekends when she slept late, finally got up and performed some chores around the house, then headed to the bar.

Adam hadn't had the chance to see her much. The Caraway clan kept him busy sewing up fresh wounds, and having medical emergencies down at the mansion. So while the Baileys watched their daughter slowly kill herself, the world kept turning.

The only difference about today was Ted Grand had her stay late doing inventory. The shop was dark and the streets were empty when she walked out into the brisk night. It was sharp, with a breeze that assaulted her face with the salty air off the ocean. Her nostrils flared at the scent of the salt. The town was so quiet this night. She looked up at the sky. It looked like there was a storm rolling in, but the full moon was shining, leaving plenty of light to walk home by.

She took a deep breath. The smell was getting to her here. Every time she breathed in, memories from her former life tried to creep into her consciousness. She didn't want them: they gave her a false sense of security. Security didn't exist. Whenever she felt comfortable, something always changed for the worse. She had learned that lesson hard.

She could see the lights of the bar from the shop, and she stopped and stared as she finished locking the doors. She knew her parents were going to send her away. They didn't have to tell her: it was in the way her mother wouldn't look at her, the way her father stayed at work as much as he could, the way David stared at her with those pleading puppy eyes.

She couldn't be the person they wanted her to be. She was fragile, and she was powerless. The wind caught her hair and swept it toward the ocean. She looked down at the coast she had been avoiding all this time.

Why? She wondered to herself. *Why should I avoid the ocean?* Nothing mattered now. Soon her parents would send her to a padded cell where nothing would change. The doctors would try to talk to her, pretend they understood, and then put her on drugs.

She thought of the story Adam had told her on that night several months ago and looked up at the full moon again. Her feet began to move, and before she knew it she was standing on the unkempt, rocky shore of the beach. The angry waves were curling around her feet; it was cold and it was refreshing. She closed her eyes, turning her face up toward the moon. Another person would have thought the night was magical, but Alice felt nothing.

Tears rolled down her face. The water circled her knees, her ill-fitting khakis soaked.

"Once upon a time I was a great swimmer, and I found peace whenever I was in the water," she whispered to the night. The wind picked up in response, as if it was urging her forward. She closed her eyes, feeling the water caressing her calves. The waters were choppy here, but she knew it wouldn't be a problem for a strong swimmer like her. She looked out at the water. She wanted to feel it embrace her again. She had always felt safe in the water. The water was the one place she knew what to do.

She began to strip off her clothes already soaked from the spray off the waves. In the moonlight, anyone looking could have seen the contours of her body. Her skin was so pale from being indoors that she almost glowed in the moonlight. During the day, she purposefully wore mostly men's clothes, baggy t-shirts and cargo pants. She didn't care. She didn't want to be pretty. Beauty was a curse; it was how she landed in so much trouble. But here, in the dark, she didn't have to hide her body. The moon lit up the fading marks across her stomach and the massive scar across her right side, just below the ribcage, where once she had felt the sting of a blade. It didn't matter; all of that would disappear in the water and the only creatures that would see would be the fish.

She moved into the water, her clothes left in a pile on the beach. She thrilled as the water swirled around her midsection, hiding her scars beneath the waves. With one more deep breath, she was in. Alice was swimming, reliving the good memories of being in water. She even managed a sad little smile. When Alice smiled, all the beauty she hid became painfully visible. With this smile you wanted to weep for days. You could see the trauma she failed to hide deep within. The water was cold beneath the surface. Her breaths were sharp and her eyes wide.

Right after it all happened, when she came home from her grandmother's, her parents had sent her to several psychiatrists. It had been a waste of money. Every session she had, she sat there, immovable. She wouldn't speak a word. She had never spoken to anyone about what had happened to her. It was probably a psychiatrist that had suggested that they move to Australia. Alice didn't care. It hadn't done her parents any good, and she only let the water embrace her now as a farewell to it. They would keep her locked away forever, she knew; the things she had seen weren't something you could just get over. Eventually, maybe she would be able to hold a job and live on her own, but it would only ever be going through the motions. It didn't matter.

She let the water lift her and set her down, let the waves carry her further and further from shore, let the water wash away some of her memories. For a few moments she felt happiness, so far from the shore that she was also far from the pain she carried on her shoulders. For mere moments, the scars that went deeper than her skin were soothed. Alice owned the surface of the ocean, she pierced waves and took her quick breaths of air. She was safe here, far from the people who wanted her to be something she wasn't anymore. She could stay out here forever, just let the water carry her away to some distant shore where maybe she could start a life away from everyone she knew, by herself.

She hadn't gone swimming in a long time. She was tired. She didn't want to go back to the shore but she knew she had better. She stopped treading water for a moment, staring at the distant shore. She took a deep breath of the air and began her swim back.

A sudden twinge screamed up her leg, a painful spasm. The pain ran through her, making her yelp a mouth full of salt-water. For a moment she panicked. She stole a glance at the shore, but it was far away still. She was alone; even the moon had hidden itself behind the clouds. She tried to force her cramped leg to behave the way it should but it wouldn't. It had been too long since she had gone swimming, and now she was caught. It had happened in seconds, and she knew it was the end. She had made the mistake of feeling comfortable for one second. The water began to pull her under, embracing her, holding her tightly the way Greg once had, forcing her against her will.

It was too dark. She surfaced again, coughing and

sputtering. She couldn't see under the water, but it wasn't just the water. Something had wrapped around her leg, but she couldn't see what had her caught, and couldn't get away. She couldn't see the shore, she couldn't see any lights. She screamed again only to swallow more salt water. There was no one there anyway; no one would hear her scream, too far. Tears fell down her face. She knew this, she knew how it worked; now that she had found peace, her bad luck had found her. She couldn't dislodge her foot. She couldn't get away. She felt a second cramp crawling up her other leg. She went under again, closing her eyes.

This is it, she thought. *This time it has me.* She was resigned to it. *It's better this way. It will be easier for everyone. No one will have to send me away. They will mourn me and then they will move on, and I won't have to.* She let go, she was sinking. Shutting out the sounds was easy, there was nothing but the smell of fish and saltwater. No light, it was appropriate. All she had to do was let go, let her darkness take her away from everything.

Suddenly, she felt something slimy against her leg, like a huge fish but accompanied by an electric shock. Her eyes shot open but she saw nothing. Blinking the salt water away, she realized she was also blinking away strange pus, and it burned. It could have been anything: shark, octopus, any sea creature that haunted the night. It didn't matter. *Just let me die in peace,* she thought.

The next thing she saw was the last thing she expected. Her

view through the water was becoming clearer, and there was electricity running through her. It itched, it hurt, it burned, and here she was face to face with the irritated, stylish blond from the diner, the man she knew now as Finn Caraway.

His eyes were filled with anger, with outrage, as she continued to sink. Now she was struggling. Her calm of moments before wasn't even a memory. Alice was caught. She still couldn't move, she was burning, and she wanted to move now; she had to get away from him. Around his bare chest was a leather strap, that strap was designed to hold a knife. He had a knife, a knife. She watched with terror as he pulled it out. Her eyes got less blurred each time she blinked, but she didn't want to see. Finn moved below her, out of her sight. She wanted to scream but she was far underwater. She tried to kick at him with her good leg. Then suddenly, she was free. Every time she blinked, she saw something different, as if curtains were lifting, as if she was clearing dirt from her eye. She needed air, but the surface was so far away now. Alice was not in the world she knew, not anymore. Why had she swum so far? Her mind was pulling away from her.

She was losing coherence, she needed air but she couldn't get up, the surface it was just so far. Finn was still there, he was staring at her like she was some kind of idiot. Faintly, she wondered why he didn't need to surface. She hadn't seen or heard him on the water. Her eyes, green like seaweed caught in sunlight, were going dark.

Finn moved toward her. She was still trying to move away, but she couldn't move anymore. He stared at her. All she needed to do was breathe. Her eyes were so frightened and growing darker with the instant. She didn't understand what was happening, and she was still holding her breath. Her panic was palpable to the man. He spun in the water and smacked her in the chest with his tail. He watched the bubbles as her remaining air was released from her lungs.

He was swimming and he was staring. Why wasn't he saving her if he could swim so well? She closed her eyes, shut out the sounds, shut out the smells, shut out the light, breathe…breathe…breathe? She was breathing.

Chapter 5

Under the Sea

The girl stared groggily at Finn's tail, hardly realizing that she suddenly had one, too. He was swimming away from her. Whatever she did was her choice now, Finn didn't care. He had no desire to take care of her. He had seen her floundering and had intended only to cut her leg loose from the bit of trash that was dragging her down. Unfortunately, it turned out that this American had the gene, the one that made it possible for her to transform, despite the fact that she had been raised human. He hadn't seen or heard of a transform the past two generations but there she was, staring after him, completely and utterly lost in her new body. He would send someone else back for her. She wouldn't drown, after all. She could be someone else's problem, not his.

Behind him, Alice took deep breaths underwater water, somehow filling her lungs not with water but with air. It was insane. It wasn't possible! She stared after Finn, after Finn's tail, a tail propelling him powerfully through the water. As the nocturnal creatures of the ocean swirled about, she could see them as if it were day. *Not possible.* The words pounded through her head. She must be either delirious or dead. She blinked repeatedly and the world was clear around her. She began tentatively moving in the water. She saw her own tail. She still felt the electricity running through her body, or was that the electricity she was creating herself? This wasn't real, it couldn't be.

She screamed. It was strange; it traveled through the water, half scream, half song. Finn stopped in his tracks and turned to look at her. If he was the type inclined to laugh, her predicament would have caused him to, but he wasn't laughing, it wasn't funny. He knew that this would turn on him for the worse. A transform, after all this time? He didn't need another maid chasing him. All Finn ever wanted was to be left alone. A shark noticed her and spun away from a scent he recognized. The girl watched horrified, unable to grasp what was happening. He sighed.

Finn started back, against his better judgment. She stared at him, her eyes wide and green while she struggled to use a tail she was unfamiliar with. He stared at her for a minute. She was pathetic. Her eyes were filled with terror.

"*Help me.*" She silently pleaded with her eyes, yet she also moved away from him.

He stared at her and began to circle her. She watched him warily, but it took a couple of passes before she realized that he wasn't doing it to mock her, but to show her how to use her muscles to move her fin. She looked back at her own tail, then began imitating him, first carefully, then more confidently. The sensation of having only one limb in the water was strange to her. Was she going to be like this forever? No, she had seen Finn on land, seen him with legs. He turned to swim, and she began following. She looked backward, then turned her head again. He had stopped in front of her too close.

She reeled backwards, moving in the way he had shown her, slapping him in the chest with her fin. He narrowed his eyes at her as he moved back in the water. She was moving. That was all that mattered, right? Alice folded herself in the water, touching the very end of her new fin. The surface was strange, slimy. How had it happened to her?

She looked back up to find Finn already swimming away again. She puzzled for a moment. He obviously didn't want anything to do with her, but what kind of person stranded someone in the middle of nowhere in her situation? She had to make her decision quickly; he was moving fast, his body sluicing through the water like a bird flies through the air.

She could hear sounds, calls in the water: whales, far off. She didn't want it, she didn't want any of this. She couldn't even handle being human and now she was a mermaid? *No, I can't let this be.* She thought, *No, shut out the sounds, shut out the smells, shut out the light*...She cried into the depths of the water. She let the sound of her mantra out, let the emotion fly. Little did she know that all transforms expressed themselves in this way, but no two songs were the same. But hers was so sad, so dark.

"*Stop it.*" He said, in her head, turning around where he was far off. His eyes flamed furiously, she could see that clearly enough. She stopped. She felt the gills in her mouth and nose filtering air from the ocean. She felt the water press around her, a world she didn't know, couldn't know, but it was safe, it was warm, it was perfect. She found her calm. Looking around her, she saw everything, her mouth hanging open. There were several large predators about. She watched the octopus move on the ocean floor. The shark that had passed her was looking for food, but not her. Alice wasn't prey. She looked up, up at the surface that had seemed so far away only moments ago. She moved upwards, minute adjustments pushed her up faster than she could have imagined. She broke the barrier and the air was all around her. She breathed deep as she hung for moments in the air, arcing above the surface of the water the way the dolphins did. It burned for a second, but she felt the gills adjust, and they flapped closed, reopening when she slipped back under the waves.

Finn grabbed her and the breath fled from her lungs. He was furious and the look in his eyes terrified her. She tried to struggle, but his grip was firm. She looked at him with her bright green eyes, her long, flat hair going every which way. She stared with fear at his hand around her arm. He broke the contact as suddenly has he had come, grimacing like he had touched something filthy. As he swam away again, she got his message. Obviously, he didn't want her to do that, to be airborne, to be seen.

Finn was tired of correcting her, wanted to leave her behind for good. He had swum too far from the others, and too close to the public shore, and now he was paying for it in spades. There was no one nearby, no one to deal with this but him. What gave this crazy girl the right to be out in the ocean late at night anyway? She was about as smart as a snail to have done that with a storm coming in. But there was nothing to it; she would have to come with him. He swam forward and looked back. There she was, stupidly watching him. He swam forward and looked back again expectantly. This time she understood, and as he swam forward again, he didn't need to look back. He could hear the swish of her tail as she followed him.

Alice saw wonders of which a human could only dream. It was surreal but it was reality, she couldn't deny it. Her mind could never dream up the sights she was seeing as she followed Finn's tail. Part of her hated it, hated that she could breathe, that she could see, that she was still alive.

As far as Finn went, he was more irritable in person than he ever looked in the little diner. His movements making it clear that he didn't care one bit about her, whether she was following him or not. He headed down, down further than any person could go, into the darkness no human eye could penetrate. It unnerved her as she felt the increasing pressure around her, but Finn didn't stop. She quickly noticed that, while she could feel the difference in pressure, it wasn't hurting her. On the contrary, it felt like an old friend was holding her closer and closer. She was certain it was enough pressure to crush a human in an instant, but not her. She wasn't a human anymore.

A giant eye moved past her, beak and tentacles followed. The creature wasn't at all unnerved by Alice, but she was uneasy, and astounded at the strangeness of it. The giant squid moved on quickly and Alice had to work to catch back up to Finn. Her muscles were screaming, but she knew she would be lost without him, as terrible a guide as he was. He had passed the giant squid with as much attention as she would have given an ant.

She heard the music quite suddenly and completely unexpectedly. Like the mellow sounds of a cello, the notes moved toward her through the water. So many voices, so much sound, so much mystery; it was speaking to her. It was hard to decipher. She wasn't even sure that she could hear it all. An eerie light appeared ahead and Alice knew that they were nearing a city. Hollowed stalagmites rose from the ocean floor. It almost looked like a pueblo, but the rocks of this formation were natural. The passageways and holes, however, looked like they had been carved by hands. The area was lit with eerie sources of light which seemed to sparkle all around her. When she looked closely, she realized that there were tiny creatures that were accounting for the light. Some predators, some prey; so much life teemed around her and the music in her head pounded and called to her.

As she could see the creatures, so, too, she saw the other mer. The mer were the source of the songs. Each note she heard was pure emotion, and all the notes combined to tell a story. It was their language, and it was wonderful. Alice knew intuitively that this music was the reason so much life was drawn to the area. Even she felt stronger, in a way, nourished by the sounds.

She looked back at Finn. His eyes were darker, this light softened them a little. This time he was actually telling her to follow him. Not in the way the others were talking, but using the simple gesture that any human would use. She stared at him for a moment, wondering why none of this, in all its glory, touched him. He was growing more irritated every moment that she took to pause. Regretfully, she moved to follow the mer.

She swam beside him in silence. She was nervous around so many, swimming by, watching her, watching him. She watched around her as if she was surrounded by the most exquisite jewels on the planet. She watched in a guarded way, a way that only someone who's seen horrors can understand. He swam through one of the holes and inside waited a female. She was an older mer, and she was rather large. Outside she hadn't seen many mer that had weight on them, but this woman made up for all of that. She looked at Finn with a smile, a smile tinted with sadness, but friendly and boisterous all the same.

She stared at Alice in a way that made her feel underdressed. There was her bra and there was her tail, she threw her arms across her belly to hide her scars, only now realizing that they were exposed.

Finn pointed at Alice, saying *"She's your problem now,"* as he left her with the older woman.

The fat mer nodded respectfully, and Finn turned tail and left in a huff. He was out of sight before Alice even registered the fact that he had left. She was alone with the large woman and felt immensely compromised by the entire situation. She had thought she would go for a little swim alone and now she was in the midst of a city, surrounded by strange creatures she had never seen, some transparent and glowing, others were mermaids; mermaids, something that wasn't even supposed to exist at all. Oddly enough, the mer seemed the most likely of creatures she could see outside the little city.

The fat mer was staring at Alice again, looking her up and down, judging her.

"Forgive me, it's been so long."

Alice flinched. She heard the voice in her head, though she saw the woman's lips move all the same. The woman didn't change her gaze. *"A transform with mine own eyes. I never thought I'd see the day."* The woman's gaze changed, and looked beyond Alice. Alice spun in the water awkwardly, only to catch the briefest glimpse of a small face staring the same way the fat mer did. Alice looked back at the fat one. *"They call me Misa. Keeper of records for what remains of this clan."*

"How?"

The staring, it was bothering her. Alice spun again, only to see several more tails disappearing. There were people watching her. She turned her face again, and Misa was in front of her, reaching for her hands. She balked at the gesture. Misa jerked her offer of comfort back, regarding the transform.

"How and why are human conundrums. Here, we simply have life." Misa said, her eyes falling to rest upon Alice's scars. Alice's eyes paled and she disappeared into her mind. Life. That was something she had been avoiding for a long time. Now she had a new one that she wanted no more than she wanted the first one.

"Your name."

Alice stared at the mer, at the way her fat melted into her tail. She heard the sigh come from the woman's mouth as a song. The mer regarded Alice. She turned and gestured to Alice to follow. Alice followed Misa dutifully. She couldn't think of what she would do or where she would go. The tunnel they went down was dark, and the way ahead was filled only by the girth of the mer.

Alice stopped as the tunnel opened up into a vast cavern. In spite of herself, her mouth gaped again. It was a grotto as large as a football field, filled with marks, drawings, names. She couldn't even see where the roof of the grotto lay, but inside the cavern sparkled. Misa was smiling at her knowingly. Alice swam along the walls, ignoring the three other mer in the room to look at some of the drawings. She touched a carving of a mer that had to be countless years old.

"The water can destroy but it can preserve as well." Misa was right next to her, Alice hadn't even noticed. *"Your name."*

Alice looked up at the woman's kindly face. She put a

tolerable distance between them as she noticed the gap mouthed stares of the other mer in the room.

"Alice Bailey"

"Ah. I'll have Aria take you home." Misa began to sing and several other mer took up the call. Alice listened to the song echo around her, it was as if it was calling to someone. When she turned around, the wide-eyed little mer was staring at her.

She was a little girl with a strong tail and wide brown eyes. Her small gangly hand reached out to touch Alice's face. Alice jerked back before forcing herself to let the girl touch her. She smiled a sweet little smile before moving away so fast that Alice could hardly keep up. The girl swam back and motioned for Alice to follow her with a huge smile on her thin little face.

Alice had so much trouble keeping up with the little girl in the water, and she was so weary. She didn't want to think about any of this now. She didn't even want to be a part of her own people, let alone a whole new society. Alice's world had just gotten a bit more complicated, and she really didn't need it. The little girl was way too happy, and by the time Alice broke the surface again, she landed on a soft beach, breathless.

The little girl was already running into the large mansion on the beach, her quick little tail transformed into quick little feet instead.

The mansion loomed huge over the beach in the moonlight.

The storm had strewn debris all over the beach, but the worst of it had petered out. Her tail flopped in the surf. She had followed the girl, she knew where she was, but not what to do, and the mansion was extremely imposing. It felt like the giant windows looking out on the ocean were staring at her. They were so dark and she couldn't see through them. All Alice wanted to do was lay her head down, close her eyes, just...

The girl poked at her with a towel, looking at her insistently. "What am I supposed to do?" Alice demanded a little too strongly, surprised to hear her own voice again. Aria jumped.

"Your tail will disappear when you are dry," the girl explained, looking at her feet uneasily. Alice moved herself up further on the beach.

"This is the Caraway mansion," Alice said, looking up at those dark empty windows.

"Y-yes," replied the little girl, twiddling her thumbs.

"Shouldn't I be getting shot?"

The girl gave her a wide eyed stare in response "Y-yer onea us." Aria said, as if that answered all questions.

It didn't answer any questions for Alice, and she stared astounded as her tail melted into her legs. The pressure of what she now knew, and how much she didn't know, began to pound at her head. She looked up, only to see the little girl launching herself into the ocean and swimming away.

The night around her was quiet, as calm as her body was in turmoil. She never should have stepped into the water. She forced herself to her unsteady feet, wrapping the towel modestly around her. Every move she made felt like she was moving through molasses, even though the air against her skin felt light as a feather. Her muscles were bruised and beaten. It was a feeling she was all too familiar with.

Alice's tail was gone, but she knew it was there lurking, waiting to emerge, waiting make her life worse than it already was. She walked through the sleeping town. She felt like a stranger. The night didn't seem like night anymore, she could see through the darkness. The bar was closed and quiet, the town was sleeping, no one noticed the girl in a towel forcing herself through the streets at night.

She made it home by early morning, finally. She crept as quietly into the house as she could, feeling more exhausted than she had in a long time. She tiptoed across the wooden floor and into her room; the sky was lightening out the tiny window above her bed. She tossed the towel into a corner and peeled off her wet and ruined bra. She forced herself to put on her pajamas, if only to feel the comforting warmth of the cotton against her skin. The next thing she knew, she was falling into the bed, dragging the covers over her, winding herself in them like a cocoon as her head hit the pillow.

It almost felt as if she were there again down in the ocean

with the blankets so tightly wrapped around her, it was comforting and it was vile at the same time but Alice couldn't care less. As she slipped into sleep she could hear her father stirring, which would make it at least five o'clock in the morning. The waves of sleep pulled her down into their depths.

Chapter 6

Day One

It was so dark and so cold. The water from above poured down on Alice's face. She looked to the side and saw her grandmother's face and the fear in her eyes. Bright green eyes, just like Alice's. Suddenly it wasn't her grandmother she was looking at, it was herself. She was floating in the water, she was safe. The dark monster from the shadows was there. He was beating at the glass. He was trying to get to her to take his knife and plunge it there in her side, right below her ribcage. She looked down. The scar wasn't there anymore…but a tail was.

He was stabbing at the glass – or was it ice? – separating them with a knife. She couldn't even be sure she was in that parking garage anymore. For once, Alice was completely confused instead of terrified. *This is a dream, isn't it?* she wondered to herself. Out of the shadows another figure walked, naked and beautiful.

She walked with an exotic swing to her hips. Her hair was long and black, and her eyes were so dark they might as well have been black, too. Alice wanted to scream at her, "No! He'll hurt you: you're naked!" Not a word escaped her mouth, and the woman kept walking forward. There was a hairnet woven into her hair: sea grass and pearls. The woman was small, but her body was strong. Looking back at Alice, she lifted her finger to her lips. *Shhhh.* Alice heard the sound purr around her in the waters of the ocean, held back only by that thin layer of glass. Suddenly, a chink flew out and the ocean began to drain slowly into the dark parking garage as Brassila advanced on the monster.

His eyes were red as he tried to get at Alice. Behind him, Brassila reached up into her hair to retrieve a blade from hair cascading tresses. It shone in the darkness as the hairnet slipped soundlessly into the water pooling at her bare feet.

Brassila wrapped her arms around the unsuspecting monster and Alice watched him struggle against her. Brassila slid the blade across his throat and blood poured into the water. The woman let go of his body carelessly, letting the dying man slide to her feet as she stepped closer to the glass. She reached out, slamming the hilt of the dagger against the wall of ice.

The ice crumbled into a thousand shining pieces and Alice found the water carrying her toward the decorative knife, but before she knew it, the knife was gone and Brassila's open arms were embracing her.

They were sitting on the beach together, waves lapping against them, Alice lying in Brassila's lap. But then it wasn't Brassila anymore, it was her grandmother. Her grandmother sat with her tail stretched out toward the sea, cradling Alice's head in her arms. Alice could smell the deep briny salt as the waves caressed them both.

"Grandma?" She smelled her grandmothers' smell, a smell so familiar, and yet so recent; it was also the smell of the cavern below the waves.

"My dear," her grandmother replied, smiling at her with that vaguely sad smile Alice knew so well. "You are stronger than you know."

"I couldn't do anything. It was Brassila who saved you."

"Was it?" Her grandmother raised her eyebrows. Alice looked down at her hands where she clenched the shining dagger. Her grandmother reached forward and took the dagger from Alice's hands, sheathing it in the hairnet Alice wore in her long, unkempt blond hair. Alice reached back and felt it with astonishment, somehow knowing it would be there: the smoothness of the pearls, the taut strands of seaweed woven between them. She looked up at her grandmother, astonished. Her grandmother smiled proudly. "My little Aly." She leaned down and kissed Alice on the forehead. "It's time to wake up."

Alice woke up with the sun pouring across her face, warming her cheek. Blinking, she realized David was sitting in the chair next to her bed, his DS laying on her nightstand. He was watching her with curiosity bordering on concern.

"What are you doing here?" she mumbled groggily. Her

head felt heavy, like she had spent the entire night drinking. Every muscle in her body screamed with the pain of an intense workout. She put her hand to her head trying to steady the spinning sensation and focus on her brother instead of her aches and pains.

"I saw you come in last night," David said, suspiciously, as she slowly sat up. She looked at him, her green eyes cloudy as usual. Though David still wasn't sure how it happened, he knew that the girl who came back from Grandma's after the funeral wasn't has sister anymore. She had gone somewhere else and no one could reach her anymore. David was the one who tried to reach her most, but even he was starting to wonder if it was hopeless. But he wouldn't let himself give up. He hated the fact that their parents didn't seem to do anything about her. They just let her slip away from him, from her friends, from the world.

"You were on the computer," she finally said, a statement instead of a question. He looked sheepish. She had put him on the defensive, trying to drive him away. She did it so often now, it was a habit, but David just couldn't get used to it.

"It was a Friday night and I didn't have any homework. It's not like there's anything else to do in this podunk town."

"No." Alice responded hazily.

He stood suddenly, angrily, "At least I'm not out all night drinking, making everyone around me miserable." He stalked away. His insult didn't even touch her. She had grown such thick skin, like ice. She threw the covers back and stood, ever so slowly, wincing as she put her bare feet to the floor. She must have stepped on so many rocks coming home, but only now did she have realize that she had come home without shoes.

David slammed the door to his room, the bang soon followed by the sounds of combat, a computer game turned up as loud as he dared without making Mom scream at him. Sarah came up the stairs, biting her tongue when she noticed the video game soundtrack, then deciding to ignore it this time. She was coming to make sure her daughter was getting dressed; when Alice didn't have work, sometimes she would just lie in bed staring at the wall, and they had made a pact that she would at least put clothes on every day. Before she got to her daughter's door, Alice emerged, walking stiffly and wearing her flannel pajamas and carrying a towel Sarah didn't recognize, disappearing quickly into the bathroom.

Though her body was moving stiffly, Alice's mind wanted to run, just run, until her legs gave out on her or she reached the edge of some cliff. She settled for shutting and locking the bathroom door. The familiar bottle of aspirin in the medicine cabinet was almost empty, but she dropped a few in her palm and threw them back. She stared at herself in the mirror before turning on the shower. Her face looked sallow, her cheeks and eyes sunken into her pale skin. She turned away quickly.

Stepping into the burning water, Alice let it ease the soreness out of her body, waiting for the aspirin to kick in. She stared down at her feet, which were still feet. Was there really a tail there, waiting to appear? If so, when would it? *Probably when you least want it to,* she thought.

It was noon when she left the shower. Her wet hair hung in a clump behind her head, carelessly dripping on the floor as she walked to David's room. He didn't turn from his computer; he didn't need to see that face. Sometimes, Alice looked like she was dead, even as she walked around. He didn't want to see it, and he didn't want her to see his face scrunched up so he could stop the tears from falling from his eyes.

"Where's mom?"

"She went to get groceries," he said.

Alice turned away without another word, and David let her go without a fight.

As Alice slipped her pants over damp skin she realized just how hungry she was. Her stomach rumbled as she crept down the stairs and made a trip to the empty fridge. She sighed, grabbed her purse and decided to go to the diner instead. David heard the front door shut and knew she was going out and hadn't even thought to tell him where.

The walk to the diner was uneventful, the sun blaring in her eyes. She stared at the ground, letting her hair in fall of her face, hiding from the smiles and stares of the townies. It was maddening: some seemed more friendly, some just watched her, but none of them were interested in who she was. She remembered walking down the street with her grandmother, disarming people with their friendly smiles and waves. Unfortunately, that attitude hadn't really served Alice very well. In truth, it was part of what had destroyed her. She saw the glass breaking in her dream again, and the intense gaze of Brassila, and she shivered.

She walked through the doors of the diner and moved quickly to a booth in the dark corner, out of the way of people coming in. As far from people as she could be in the public diner.

"I'll take a Caesar Salad," Alice said to the waitress carelessly. She slunk back into the corner as far as she could, hoping that no one would see her. She stared at the wall, trying to puzzle through the night before.

She was in the middle of her salad when four girls slid into the booth with her. She looked up with surprise. The dark-haired girl sitting next to her shoved her. Alice felt the shock run through her, and she knew. They were the fashionable girls, the same ones that had been gathered around Finn the first week she had arrived in this forsaken town. The quick shock told her that they also happened to be mer. She looked at them around her, the pushy dark-haired girl beside her and three on the opposite bench: a blond vacant one, a shy little redhead looking uncomfortable pressed against the wall, and the one in the middle, with the sickly sweet smile, and brown hair with blond highlights.

"Ashley was right. This girl doesn't even have a prayer,"

said the blonde, swiping hair from her eyes.

The redhead looked at Alice with curiosity; "She's the first transform in a century…" she trailed. Alice avoided her blue eyes. What did they want from her anyway? Alice didn't think she was being unclear about not wanting to be a member of their club.

"As long as she doesn't think that makes her special," said the girl in the middle, clearly the leader. "We're here to welcome you," she said to Alice.

"What's your name?" the redhead asked, seeming genuinely friendly. Alice looked at her, but made no move to respond.

"Quiet, Kari, this isn't a meet and greet, this is business. Alice, you are of age and you need to know some of our rules," the leader began again.

"You are to talk to none of us, you are one of us but you are not on the same level as us. Certainly you will have males pursue you, being the first transform in a while. You are not to chase a male. You are dirty, half-human."

Alice stared at her. What was this girl talking about? Because the first thing Alice wanted anything to do with was guys. She had never "chased a man" in her life, and she wasn't about to start. She had a feeling that they just wanted Finn to themselves. This was some kind of intervention. That was fine, they could have him; it was obvious to her that this was how they passed their time, chasing after a guy who wanted nothing to do with anyone, as far as she had noticed.

Alice knew she was being manhandled; one of her psychiatrists had tried to do the same, and he had gotten the same reaction as this clique. Alice picked up her fork, looked down at her meal and began to eat again, ignoring them with the hope they would just go away. She hadn't reacted to anything for years now; there was no reason to change her routine for these annoying girls.

"Now that that's all clear, let me introduce everyone." said the girl across the table in a fake-sounding voice, flipping her streaked brown hair and ignoring the fact that Alice was ignoring her. "I'm Ashley. Everything that happens in our clan goes through me, and you can feel free to ask me anything you want. These others are the unmated women of Brassila's clan: Ilse," she pointed to the blonde, "Carmen," Alice felt another shock from the one beside her. "And Kari the Selkie," Ashley finished, motioning offhandedly to the redhead next to her. Briefly, Alice's eyes found the redhead's, clearly the meekest, with an odd title. Alice had no idea what any of it meant nor did she really care. She continued to eat silently.

Across from Alice, Ashley was getting slightly annoyed. She hadn't expected to be ignored by the transform. "You don't have a human lover, do you?" Ashley asked, trying to get the transform's attention. In that task, she was failing miserably. Alice stared at the Formica table, chewing each bite carefully, just hoping that the intrusion would disappear. Ashley's smile turned sour. "Who are we kidding? You couldn't attract a man of any species."

Ilse laughed, Carmen shocked her, and Kari looked like she'd rather be somewhere else. Alice flinched at Carmen's touch. She looked like the oldest there, and yet it wasn't hard to tell that she was completely under Ashley's thrall. Ashley commanded obeisance, and the more Alice ignored her the more it irked the mer. Alice was starting to wonder if she could get them to go away. She finally looked up at Ashley, her irritation apparent, her teeth grinding at the shocks she was receiving from the mer next to her.

"What do you want?" Alice asked coldly.

"It's unlikely you'll attract a mate, but I just want to be clear with you," Ashley reiterated. "You are of an eligible age, but you're to stay away from the man who turned you. You will not be going after the prize stallion." Alice almost choked, almost laughed, but she restrained herself, not wanting to dignify Ashley with a response. She didn't care about what the girl was saying, didn't care about her little world. Alice simply stared at Ashley, challenging her unwittingly with her silence.

Ashley's face darkened, but Alice wasn't really looking at her, only through her, the way she looked at everyone.

"Finn belongs to one of us, the loyal ones, the true bloods. If you make any move toward him, we will smear you against a boat and make hats of your fins," she said menacingly, lowering her voice. Alice raised her eyebrows. Ashley smiled again and began to talk normally. "Not that you would. I mean you wouldn't stand a chance anyway; you're just so darn ugly." Ashley laughed and her posse followed suit.

"Let me help you understand," Alice hissed, "I want nothing to do with your politics and your people. I just want to be left alone." Ashley stared at her. Little did she know that it was the first time Alice had spoken to defend herself in a long time. Alice's head was filled with images of the knife crashing through the glass, the knife in her hand, the face of her grandmother, but Alice's gaze remained steadily on the mer. Carmen and Ilse looked to Ashley for a lead, and Kari looked out the window, looking like she couldn't decide if she wanted to flee or to say something.

"We only want to help. It can't be easy." Kari put in suddenly. Ashley spun in her seat and shoved Kari into the wall. Kari winced. Alice returned to her food as if nothing had happened.

"You're here because we let you be here, too, Selkie," said Ashley to the red-head. She turned back to Alice, who didn't even deign to look up again. "Be careful, transform; you certainly don't want to make the wrong enemies." She turned to her posse, "Come on, ladies. Let's go. I think she's got the message." She shoved Ilse out of the way as she exited the booth. Carmen turned and gave Alice one last shock for good measure as they all flounced out of the diner. Alice's nostrils flared and she felt a burn as, for a split second, her gills let in pure air.

Something about the girl with her stylish clothes and her stylish make-up calling her ugly bothered her faintly. Alice felt strangely warm; she assumed it was anger. She hadn't felt anger in a long time. She was mildly annoyed that she was angry at such high-school behavior. She stared at her food in a distant way. Maybe it would disappear without her touching it, too.

The bell on the door rang. A young man with sloppy dark blond hair walked into the diner. He spotted Alice immediately, though she was sitting in one of the furthest booths. He moved awkwardly, as if he weren't used to walking, and slid into the seat across from her without asking. He wasn't really concerned with how Alice looked; he was more interested in building a family. He noticed that there was a little color in her face, which was mildly pleasant, more than he had hoped for from the stories he had already heard of the homely transform.

The boy looked like a nerd, and she doubted that he had spent much time outside his watery home. He reached forward, brushing his hand against hers, which was still holding the fork. He sent a tingle through her that would have been pleasant to anyone that wasn't Alice. He let his hand linger on hers, hoping to feel a bit of warmth from her. He knew she wouldn't be used to their ways, how sometimes they used their electrical field to communicate, but he had expected some kind of immediate reaction.

Alice stared at his unmoving hand. She had been too slow, hadn't pulled away, and now here he was, touching her. Was it so hard to just be left alone? Alice bristled, the boy jerked his hand away, and the lights in the diner flickered. The boy glanced up worriedly, but no one in the diner really noticed the sudden power surge.

"I didn't mean to o-offend you," he said, stumbling over words he wasn't used to saying aloud. "You can't use that much current. It's dangerous among humans." Alice stared at him sideways. What was this guy doing here, anyway?

"I-I-I wanted to bid you w-welcome. I-I thought you might…enjoy…company…a guide, maybe?" Alice just stared at him. Yes, this must be what anger felt like. It had been so long that she had felt anything, let alone anger. "Maybe we could g-go for a s-swim sometime?" he said hopefully. She shook her head slowly from one side to the other, trying once again to shake away the dream from the night before. Anger lead nowhere. In the beginning there had been more anger and sadness then her body could handle. Alice had learned to cope and replaced all emotion with a state of persistent apathy. She receded back into it now, trying to keep the breaking glass and the smell of the sea out of her head.

Kendall watched her, waiting for her to respond. He sat awkwardly for a minute, "Uh...I guess you know where to find me," he said as the silence stretched on, then stood and stumbled to the door. Alice watched him go. Finally, when she knew the men were gone, she let out a sigh and returned to her meal. The anger faded once more and she was Alice again, or at least what passed for Alice these days. She was alone again.

Alice was almost finished when the diner bell rang again. A young man swaggered into the diner. Somehow he moved in a manner as sarcastic as the expression that seemed to permanently stain his face. He nodded toward the owner behind the bar, who looked completely shocked to see him. Several other patrons watched him, curiously whispering as he walked by. The entire diner was alive with an air of surprise. All eyes followed the teenager.

The whispering of the patrons was so obvious that even Alice turned to look. At least there was one thing today that people seemed more interested in than her. The boy walking in wasn't much older than David. His hair was short but stuck almost straight up. Though he certainly resembled Finn, his features were softer and his eyes darker. He had a permanent look of amusement on his face and it didn't change as the people around him whispered. Alice heard an old fisherman behind her whispering to his wife.

"Both Caraway boys back at the same time?"

"It's not normal," his wife replied.

"Something fishy's going on," he agreed. All the whispers in the room couldn't stop Tommy from moving forward. Of course, whose booth did he come to but Alice's? Now the room was completely abuzz, wondering aloud about the long-lost teenage millionaire and the new girl from the States.

"Where could she have met him?" "Why would he be interested in her?" "Tommy's been gone for months."

It went on and on, and her headache returned as quickly as her temper.

"So you're the new girl," the boy said. She stared at him with narrowed eyes.

"What do you want?"

"Your hand, of course." He smirked, putting an open hand up on the table, offering it to her. She jerked away like it was a poisonous snake. "No? Well, now that that's done." He pulled his hand back. He was laughing at her with those dark eyes of his, and the color in Alice's cheeks became hot.

"I don't need this you, little twerp," she said fiercely. She couldn't contain her nursed anger anymore; it was bursting to escape. It was making her crazy. She felt like a cornered cat, hating so many intrusions into her previously quiet existence.

The boy sneered at her. "Yesterday I was in Okinawa when I heard a tantalizingly strange tale from home. Accounts differed, but everyone whispered the word transform. I just had to see it myself. Imagine my surprise to hear my brother was involved." He smiled that crooked smile again, "I heard the tale late last night and flipped my fin back here as quick as I could. Population counts mean nothing to a new transform."

"I don't care about your stupid story. I don't care where you were. I just want you to leave." His expression mirrored his manner.

"Finn said you were annoying. I shoulda known he only woulda said that 'cuz you were as much of a bitch as he is an ass." Alice's eyes and nostrils flared again. Anger was painful with gills. He laughed, sardonically. There wasn't a serious bone in this boy's entire body, which was not what Alice needed right now. Alice didn't know what she truly needed, but she knew it wasn't this. As her brain surged into motion, rebelling at these new facts, Alice had some semblance of life.

"There *is* something behind the clouds," he said, cryptically. He smiled as she shook. "Well, I can see that you want to be left alone. I just wanted to see the truth of the matter myself. Have a great day, Alice." He smirked at her and got up to leave as quickly as he had come. He continued smirking as he walked away, everyone staring until the diner door closed behind him.

Alice looked down at the remainder of her meal and pushed it away. She sat for a moment staring at it before sliding out of the booth and paying the check.

She moved out of the diner quickly. Escaping, she entertained the thought of running again, but it disappeared as quickly as the boy. She was headed... actually, she wasn't sure where she was headed. She just needed to get out of that diner before someone else came to harass her about one thing or another.

Walking down the sidewalk she discovered that she couldn't contain her emotions anymore; perhaps it was because she was so out of practice. She ran straight into Finn before she even knew there was someone coming toward her.

"You!" she yelled. She shoved him, shocking him full-force. Finn stumbled backwards, shock plain on his face, watching those green eyes shine through her long, long hair. He hadn't really been watching where he was going, either. He was on an important mission of his own. He stared at her violent eyes and flaring nostrils. "Keep your goddamn fan club away from me!" she shouted, shocking him again as she sped past, leaving him gaping in the road.

She was moving swiftly, and before she knew it she had broken into a run. The ocean was in front of her; it was swirling around her legs and she was screaming for all she was worth. Two people on the beach stared at her. They had been sunbathing, or picnicking; it didn't matter. She hadn't met those people yet, she didn't know if they knew her; it didn't matter. She screamed at them as they gathered their things, leaving her alone on the beach. Alice turned her screams toward the ocean, tears pouring from her eyes.

"Why?" she screamed, "Why me?" She let in a breath as she fell to her knees. The water swirled around her knees and legs, her pants were soaked. She didn't care. "Why me?" she pleaded, softly this time, as her shoulders and head slumped in exhaustion.

Out to sea and out of sight, Tommy surfaced to laugh. He could hear her scream. Unknown to her, her very human scream of frustration had an underlying tone in the language of the folk, the language she could now speak but didn't know. Alice was telling the world to "fuck off," and this underlying tone was keeping people away. He contemplated going to her, but he had a feeling she would figure things out on her own.

She screamed again. Slowly it dissolved into a whimper. Touching her face, she felt the salt water there. She was crying. She didn't know when she had started crying or when she had stopped screaming, but there they were, the tears on her face, friends she had lost long ago. Terror had been far more real to her than sadness.

Alice didn't know how long she was there, but she let her body wrack with her sobs in the surf, which gently caressed her with each swell. Wave after wave crashed against her knees. It crawled up to her midsection before she realized that she should get up. Her legs were stiff as she regained her feet, her shoes squishing with water. The tears had dried on her face and she knew exactly where she was going. She hoofed it up to the bar. The only thought on her mind was to drink herself stupid, drink until she puked all her guts out, whatever they were made of now. A few shots of heavy whiskey, certainly a couple of beers, too; beer before liquor, of course. She landed at a barstool, she wanted to be gone, she didn't want to be a part of this body or this life. Why when she wanted no part of one world was she suddenly being wound into the clutches of another, it wasn't fair and it wouldn't do.

Drink her brain told her. *Drink* it pounded in her temples.

Drink until everything goes black.

Chapter 7

Doctor Knows Best

"Oh, hell no, I want no part of this," Adam fumed. "How did it happen? What? Fuck!" He yelled at Finn. He spun toward the house. They were in old Mrs. Maygood's garden. He had been performing a house-call when Finn showed up on the doorstep. "How did you even know where to find me?"

"Natalie."

"I keep your secret, I hired one of your people, and now you have the audacity to interrupt me while working to throw your problems at me!"

"She's one of you."

"Apparently not anymore!" Adam ran his hand through his hair in frustration. "This is not my problem..." he trailed off, "God," he sighed. He knew he was going to help; there wasn't really much choice in the matter. After all, she would be one of his patients, sooner or later. He spun back toward Finn. "This is your fault; this is your job. You should be dealing with this."

"We both know I'm the worst equipped for that kind of thing," Finn said, narrowing his eyes.

"Donkey's years and you still throw it in my face; I wasn't

even your doctor then. I didn't even know then."

"Your father…"

"Knew exactly what to do: he left. He wanted nothing more to do with any of you."

"Says the man with the new yacht – bought with whose money?" Adam stared at the boy angrily. He wasn't wrong: Adam got paid for his troubles, ten-fold. Paid for his discretion.

"I have work to do; I'll find her after that. I have a feeling I know exactly where she'll be."

Adam blew through the coconut entrance to the bar. He looked at the bartender. He was still irked at Finn, but he tried to make himself appear as his smiling self. There was a sense of urgency to his pursuit by now. If she was bad off as he figured, she probably wasn't going to be getting home. Maybe he should rephrase that: he couldn't let her go home.

"The Bailey girl, she here?"

"Yep. She moved out to the wall 'bout, oh...an hour ago?" the barkeeper replied, gesturing.

"How much has she had?"

"Oh...three martinis, maybe four shots of Jack, and two grogs." He reached up and sheepishly scratched his head. "Seppo can really drink, doc."

"She all paid?"

"Nah, she's got a tab open."

"Here." Adam handed the bartender his credit card.

"Awfully nice of you, doc," said the bartender as he ran the card through the machine, then handed it back. Adam took a deep breath, then headed toward her table.

Alice didn't know where the time had gone; her brain was completely fuzzy when she looked up into Adam's face. She was on the concrete wall behind the bar. She had been watching the ocean, or the stars, or something; she didn't really remember. All she knew was that no one had bothered her – until now. Adam loomed above her, staring at her, probably trying to gauge just how drunk she was. Alice was wasted and didn't rightly care.

"Hi," he said.

"The fuck you want?" she demanded with a slur, trying to sit up and almost falling over the edge. He grabbed her arm and, supporting her, lifted her off the wall and positioned her so she sat facing him. He was doing something, touching her face, looking at her pupils; it was uncomfortable and she didn't like it. A shock ran through her body, making him jump a little.

"Hell of a day?" he asked. He was putting her arm around his shoulders. His arm snaked around her waist, lifting her. She thought about struggling, but she probably couldn't have walked right then anyway.

"Your stupid town sucks!" she answered. She sent another jolt of electricity through his arm. It didn't hurt; he knew she could do worse if she weren't so intoxicated. He smiled that good-natured, winning smile, though this one was a bit strained.

"Come on, you don't need to be here."

"You wanna take me to some cozy lil alley?" She demanded defensively, or as defensively as she could, drunk as she was.

"No," he said seriously, "I need to get you away from people."

She looked him up and down suspiciously. She didn't look good. She bent forward and in the next moment, she was vomiting. He stood over her, supporting her; trying to keep her hair out of the way.

"Come on, Miss Martini," he helped her out of the bar. "Clean-up out there," he called to the bartender apologetically, who nodded as he watched them leave with relief.

Adam kept walking as Alice sent dull shock after dull shock through his body. He moved her down toward the marina where his boat was moored. It was a decent-sized sailing yacht that could function with or without the sails. He laid her on her side in the bunk with a bucket next to her, and then went out to call her parents.

"Hello?" Sarah picked up the phone.

"Hi, it's Adam Carson."

"Are you okay, Adam? You sound out of breath."

"Alice had a little too much to drink tonight, so I wanted to let you know that she can't make it home, but she's safe." There was silence on the other end. Then he heard a sigh.

"Thank you for taking care of her."

"It's no problem." They hung up and he went back to the boat and got underway. He hadn't been honest with her mother. Surely her mother assumed Alice was safe on Adam's couch, not sailing out to sea. A drunken person on a boat wasn't usually recommended. Adam couldn't take her home, though. He couldn't put Alice in their custody without them knowing something was very different about their daughter. Late that night he fell asleep in a lawn chair on the deck, staring at the stars above, listening to the sounds of the water against the ship. It would be very soothing if it hadn't been for the sound of heaving he heard from the cabin every so often.

Alice sat straight up in a strange bed, banging a head that was already pounding. She reached one heavy, tired arm up to rub the bump as she tried to make sense of her surroundings. She smelled the heavy cigarette smoke from the bar clinging to her exceedingly wrinkled but familiar clothes. She hated feeling so unkempt, though she wouldn't admit it. She looked with slit eyes at the table next to her. There was a concoction sitting there, and a couple of what she could only assume were aspirin. She downed the foul liquid and took the aspirin, hoping the medicine would help her make sense of this strange, small room.

She lay back down and looked around carefully. There was no bucket on the floor, but she remembered one had been. Her purse was nearby, slouched by the door of a tiny bathroom. She suddenly realized that the back and forth motion was not her headache, but waves beneath her. She was on a ship. That didn't scare her much. Even in her current state, she knew that she could get away from any ship. The burn in her nose reminded her of how little she had to fear from the water now. She stood and moved toward the bathroom, where she threw some cold water on her face and filled the empty glass with some water. She felt a little better; at least she didn't feel like she was going to throw up anymore.

She moved slowly up to the deck, not sure exactly what she would find. What she found was the doctor. The anger flared in her again.

"You have some real nerve," Alice said, upon seeing Adam. He smiled at her.

"What, dragging some flailing, electric, drunk woman to my ship in the middle of the night?"

"I shocked you?" For a moment, Alice was horrified, but he seemed so calm about it.

"You should come with a warning label: handle with welding gloves, or maybe with one of those things the nature show guys use to hold giant snakes," he joked. "Bartender would have thought that was a little strange."

Alice just stared at him. That was Adam's way of explaining; Alice understood that. What she didn't understand was the doctor himself. "Are you...?"

"I'm not a mer, no," he said, turning to smile at her. It put her off her guard, the way he smiled: there was sadness in his smile, or stress, something. He laughed at her expression, at the way she watched him with suspicious eyes through her hair. His laughter broke through the air like a smashed vase; Alice stumbled backwards in response. For a moment, both just stared at each other, contemplating the other.

"Here," he finally said, tossing her an ornate belt.

She caught it, barely. It looked handmade. It seemed like leather, but it wasn't; she honestly couldn't tell what it was made from. It had a little scabbard that hid a knife, of all things. She looked at it with a strange sense of horror. The handle shone in the light, decorated with shells and shiny rocks that could have been gems. She looked back at him, eyes large with disbelief.

"Tommy was going to bring it to you. He said that he thought you might have started a scene in the diner had he given it to you then." She narrowed her eyes at him. "You had a hell of a day yesterday no?"

"You knew all along," she said flatly.

"About you? No. I knew about you only after Finn came and told me yesterday; after he had an interesting run-in with you, actually. He told me he didn't know what you were going to do, but that I should make sure you didn't risk the folk. That's why I went to the bar to find you. I didn't really have a choice in the matter."

"And what the hell is this?" she said, holding the belt out as far away from her body as she could.

"It's a knife."

"You know what I mean!"

"It's for fighting. Why do you think the town doctor has to know about the folk in the first place? They sound like silly little duels, but I'm the one who has to stitch ya'll up afterwards, and sometimes it gets bloody. After all, you think a local doctor could afford a rig like this?" Alice looked around. The boat looked brand new, and far too nice for a little-known town like Brassila Cove. It also explained why he didn't have a choice to pick her up: retrieving a drunken mermaid was simply a paycheck to him. Alice scoffed and turned away, dropping the knife onto a nearby chair. As she looked out at the sea she could smell that scent, feeling its pull on her.

"That story you told me. You knew."

"Very secretive, your new friends are. I thought you could use a little fantasy."

"Out of the blue...Brassila was a mermaid," she said calmly, reiterating what she had already known on some level. She turned back to the ocean, feeling the sun warm her skin.

"Yes. This town is here because of the mer, because of one man's crazy obsession with a particular mer." He sighed, "Look, I don't want to hold you hostage or anything. You're welcome to have breakfast with me." Alice turned back to him, surprising him with the glint of sunlight in her eyes. She looked away quickly. It looked like she wasn't used to making her eyes focus on anything. He watched her carefully. She looked toward the little booth and table. It looked comfortable. It seemed his boat was designed less for sailing and more for entertaining. "I've got orange juice and a bit of cereal," he said.

"What you're telling me is, I'm a paycheck to you, but you want to feed me breakfast anyway?" Alice wondered aloud as she slid into a seat across from him. He reached forward and poured her a glass of orange juice. She watched the juice steadily fill the plastic glass. "Why me, anyway?" He moved to get her some cereal but she put her hand up. She wasn't sure she could eat anything solid at the moment. Her head was pounding and the gulls above were screaming in her ears. He said nothing; he didn't want to interrupt the normally taciturn woman. "I mean, I go for a swim for the first time in a long time, and all of a sudden I'm trapped in the middle of two worlds! I've got girls threatening me, boys smirking at me, and a whole other set of guys coming out of the blue asking for something akin to my hand in marriage. At least, that's what I think he was doing…"

Orange juice burst from Adam's nostrils as he burst into earsplitting laughter once again. Alice stared at him, pressing herself back into the cushions of the booth.

"I'm sorry, it's just… Ashley and her sharks…" He laughed, she stared. He regretfully calmed his outburst. "It's not too uncommon that you might have that gene. What's uncommon is that you would come in contact with one of the folk. The folk have been integrating into human society for a long time: just like the Disney movie, a maid or man will fall for a human. It's sharply discouraged: when you leave the water for a human, you leave the water for good."

"You mean?"

"It's a risk the folk can't take, that one of them would expose them. So, yes, they will destroy you, one way or another, if you enter the ocean again after declaring yourself to a human."

"Why?"

"The folk are the caretakers of the ocean, the way humans are to be the caretakers of the land. I would say the folk do a much better job of it. Unfortunately, the folk are amphibious; like sea turtles, they need the land to breed, so the folk are as tied to land as they are to the water. And if they go on land…"

"They meet humans."

"And sometimes..."

"Fall in love."

"Their numbers have been diminishing for centuries. As they diminish, you see strange things, like giant clouds of mucus or strange secretions on the surface. Not that humans don't cause their share of ocean mischief." Alice sat in silence for a while, letting it all sink in, letting her brain try to reboot itself after the previous night.

She shook her head. "This is nuts. A few days ago, I thought mermaids were a fairy tale."

"Yeah, took me a while to get used to it, too. Those gills..." He idly put his hand on top of hers. It was warm and comforting, but she instantly pulled her hand away.

"Don't," she said defensively. Her eyes went wild and crazy once more.

"I'm sorry; I didn't mean anything by it," he said, then glanced away. "I know that you..."

"My father told you that something happened to me, a couple years back."

"He didn't tell me what," he said defensively. Alice stood up furiously, knocking over the glass of juice. It made her stomach lurch a little.

"I hate you. You act all concerned, but you're getting paid for it. I hate your town and its stupid secrets, and I certainly never asked for this," she said through gritted teeth.

"It's life, Alice. Yeah, it's a piece of shit, but you deal with what you're dealt. I get paid to deal with these mutants, sure, but…"

"Mutants? You're calling me a mutant now?"

"I didn't mean it that way."

"I'm pretty sure you meant exactly what you just said." Her eyes, her nose, her gills all flared at once. "You have no idea what you're talking about," she hissed. "Pompous little rich boy living high on the hog for a secret he's paid to keep. You don't know anything about hardship!"

Adam watched her in silence; he wasn't the type to get riled up. He watched the flaring intensity disappear from her eyes, watched them cloud over. For a moment, Alice was back there, back where she didn't want to be, in a place she couldn't escape. She had lost control, again. Quickly, she forced her eyes to narrow on him again, squeezing away the darkness invading her thoughts. He couldn't really understand why this concerned him at all: she was one of them now, not his problem.

He gritted his teeth: those eyes, that hopelessness. She was one of them, yet all he wanted to do was jump up and gather her in his arms. He knew that pain in her; he had seen it once upon a time in his father. It was that pain that had separated father from son. He wanted to stroke her long hair telling her that everything was okay, everything would turn out all right. Twice he had dealt with tragedy. The look in her eyes reminded him of being eight, looking up into his mother's eyes. He hadn't been able to make things better for her, but maybe he could for Alice. He stood up slowly, but Alice jumped back.

She stared at him outraged as he just stood there, staring at her like she was something he had to fix, something he could sew up and heal. Alice knew better than anyone that things wouldn't always be okay, that things always turned out dark. It would always hurt; she would always see their faces and smell the blood. She backed away from his eyes, from his body, from his concern. Grabbing the belt, she continued facing Adam until she felt the cold metal of the railing behind her. He stared at her with that noxious concern and it made her ill. She spun as fast as she could manage, jumping overboard into the enveloping ocean.

Chapter 8

My Island

She plunged into the water. It wrapped her in a cocoon of safety and warmth as she fastened the belt around her. For a few moments she just let herself float, let the world come into focus around her. The water didn't burn her eyes, she wasn't afraid of drowning: it was absolute peace. Fish swam around her, ignoring her presence in their world; it wasn't just their world, it was hers, too. The water held her like a mother would a crying child. She felt her tail spread over her legs, tearing her baggy jeans apart in the process. She unwound herself from the shreds of her pants, watching them drift away from her. She kicked her tail and swam; no direction, no pesky human concerns, just a mermaid, watching the wonders of the ocean unfold around her. This was perfection; it was magical under the ocean. Alice felt at home under the waves, away, where the sun couldn't touch her.

A pod of dolphins approached excitedly. She smiled at the dolphins and they smiled back at her. They chattered and she understood exactly what they meant. It wasn't much they were saying, mostly just, "Play with us!" Dolphins didn't seem to carry the weight of the world on their shoulders. Obliging to their pleas, she bent herself, touching the very edge of her tail with her webbed fingers. One of the dolphins swam through the loop she had created. At the last second she grabbed his dorsal fin and he carried her up and up and up toward the surface. They broke the water together, separating from each other and plunging haphazardly back underneath the waves. The dolphins cackled at this new game before noticing a school of fish. They zoomed away to begin their hunt and Alice watched them go.

After awhile, swimming on her own through the open ocean, she grew tired. Not far in front of her loomed a little island. To the ocean it was little more than a freckle on its face. It looked like the little island would almost disappear when the tide rose. Still, the spot of land managed to support two scraggly palms. In the water surrounding it, there was life everywhere. She could see the sharks circling in the shallows, seeking out either their next meal or just a cleaning service.

She let the tide carry her up onto the beach, letting her tail stick out into the water, feeling the tiny fish as the tickled past her. She turned on her back to lie in the sand, and stared up at the sky more vast even than her ocean. It was peaceful and she closed her eyes, just for a little bit. The sun was beginning to set and Alice figured she might just as easily fall asleep here, where the rays of the fading sun warmed one cheek while the sand warmed the other. She dozed in and out of consciousness for a while, seeing the dolphins and the fish behind her closed eyes. She didn't know how long she'd been there when a voice made her jump.

"You're on my island."

She jerked up, her momentary calm gone before the last syllable left his mouth. Looking up, she scowled defensively. She pulled the knife from its belt and brandished it at him. He laughed at her, but it wasn't a serious laugh. He looked her up and down from where he was perched on his arms on the sand. She was now alone in the middle of the ocean facing the last person she wanted to see, and she was a sight. She was wearing the same baggy t-shirt as yesterday, feeling lucky that it was a dark color. She had sloughed off her sweater in the middle of the ocean; it had slowed her down. Sitting awkwardly with her tail still in the water, she continued to hold out the gaudy knife.

"Certainly you don't think you could fight me with that thing," he said mockingly.

His words cut her more than his knife ever could, not that he knew or cared. She had fought and lost before. She was frozen with more emotions than she could sort out running through her all at once. Of course, he didn't notice a darn thing, or if he did he certainly didn't care what they were.

"Get lost! I was here first," she finally said.

"You can stay if you're quiet," he replied, flipping onto his back, ignoring her. His tail flopped in the water. She lunged toward him, brandishing her knife, but he easily caught her wrist and twisted it away. She dropped the knife, sudden tears coming to her eyes at the pain. He stared at her with surprise and annoyance. "Don't do that again."

Alice jerked away when he released her, picking up her pride with the knife. She reluctantly slid it back into the sheath. She didn't want to leave. It was comfortable out here before he showed up. His inherent smugness made her feel stubborn, and, though there was that part of her that wanted nothing more than to swim from him at top speed, she wasn't about to give up her little paradise based on a claim that it belonged to him. She refused to give the irritating blonde the satisfaction of scaring her away. He may have everyone else in the town in thrall but he didn't own her; no man ever would. She was reminded again of her dream and the look on Brassila's face, a face that was serene, with confidence that she could fight anything that was thrown at her. Alice tried to mimic it, but ended up with something akin to pouting as she crossed her arms over her chest and sidled away from him on the sand.

They watched the sun set, bristling at one another. Why wouldn't he go away? Alice wondered. If he claimed to hate the company of people so much, her presence should have forced him to leave a long time ago.

Finn was angry she was there at all. All the mer knew this was his island; someone should have stopped her. This was where Finn came to get away from everyone, and everyone knew it. This girl seemed to exist only to plague him, and in a completely different way from the other eligible maids. She could have made a move on him, could have slid close, forcing herself upon him, but he would have kicked her away, with his own knife, if necessary.

This transform business was difficult. She was a mer now, and subject to their rules, yet if she were to get in an accident and lose her life, she would disappear according to the human laws and people would come sniffing around the Caraway mansion in a full investigation of her disappearance. If she was subject to mer laws than she was one of his subjects, which meant that she was required to obey him, or die. That didn't make any of the other maids obey him, though, and he would not kill again. It made his head pound and his stomach churn. She lay there, smugly, arms crossed over her chest. Finally it was he who broke the silence; they couldn't just continue bristling at one another. He had never disliked a trip to his island, but he had never shared the time there with anyone.

"Why are you sad? When you sang the first time, it was sad. I've never heard someone's first song be sad."

She fumed. "It's none of your goddamn business."

"You're on my island, my territory,"

"Go jump off a cliff, you arrogant, pampered brat." He turned over on his side staring at her noncommittally. The girl did have claws, and he was at fault for turning the transform, however accidentally. She drew her blade again, but she wasn't looking at his unconcerned face. Her eyes swam with her memories.

There they were again: the horror and the dream. They

were choking the twilight air around her, tearing her head apart. She had been running from them, but they had caught her up. She knew they would. She couldn't escape her head. She remembered the knife, how she took down the man in her dream herself, not Brassila. She could feel the wet blood on her hands. She looked down at the knife.

Finn watched her slipping away; the knife was shaking in her hands. It looked…familiar. His eyes narrowed at her. Suddenly, she looked up, noticing his presence once more.

"What's your problem!?" she demanded.

"Currently, the fact that you're on my island." He paused as she stared at him angrily. "But since you asked, my grandmother's dying, and that only makes all you maids chase me more. Now I can't even find peace on my own island. What's your problem?" he asked matter-of-factly, with a twinge of bitterness and anger. He sat up further. "After all, you are on my island, and you have the gall to ask me what my problem is?"

His grandmother. For a moment, all she saw was her own grandmother's face. She had loved her grandmother. She saw her grandmother's face the way it had been the last time she had seen it: gray, blank, and staring at her with dead eyes. She blinked, clearing the images from her head.

"My grandmother died," she said. It was nowhere near what she wanted to say. She had half a mind to just leave, but somehow she couldn't. She curled up her tail, bringing knees that weren't there to her chest.

"She didn't just die." Finn replied intuitively. Alice glared at him fiercely, but she saw something different. He was watching at her, but he wasn't threatening her. He just seemed curious. Listening to her, for real, not like all the people who had only listened for her parent's money.

"No." Alice answered tenderly.

Finn watched her, the way her gaunt face, hiding in her hair, told so much more than she would admit to. He knew that look, the lost look in her eyes. Maybe he had more in common with the transform than he thought. She certainly seemed to have more depth than Ashley. Alice looked off across the blackening ocean.

"She was murdered," Alice said finally.

"You were there."

"Yes." The silence stretched between them. He looked off at the ocean, his chest rising and falling with the waves. Finn knew the girl had a story, but he wasn't about to push her. He wasn't really sure he wanted to know, anyway, and of course she wasn't going to give him a choice.

"Four hours," slowly Alice began to pour the story at the night. She wasn't even talking to him and she didn't care that he was there. She spoke to the moon just beginning to rise. "For four hours I was raped by my best friend's brother. When it was apparent I was pregnant, my parents sent me to live with my grandmother, thinking my brother wouldn't be able to handle it, wouldn't be able to understand." She sighed. "Everything was fine for a while, and things even got better. I wasn't scared of everything, and I was even starting to look forward to meet the baby growing inside me. I had forgotten how much Grandma and I got along until that one night. In the dark parking garage, there was no one there. It was so late when we walked back…then there was a man, and he was mugging us at knife-point. My grandmother started having a heart attack and I wanted to help her. He went toward me to stop me, and his knife was in my gut, so close to my baby. Everything was a blur from there. He beat me down as I tried to fight him. He took everything and ran. I watched my grandmother die from the heart attack, unable to move. I was losing blood myself, and losing the baby. I had just felt the baby kick for the first time, but now it was still. It felt like forever, me and her corpse, but they told me it was only four hours."

Alice's voice faded as she remembered her head lolling to the side of the stretcher, the lights of the ambulance shining on the black body bag. In one day, she had lost her grandmother and her daughter.

There were tears pouring from the girl's eyes. Finn knew she wasn't talking to him; he felt no need to respond.

Alice had lost consciousness after, then woke to the sounds of them asking her name, where she was from. Suddenly there were so many people: cops, nurses, doctors, psychiatrists and finally, her parents. She didn't want to talk to a single one of them. If she never heard 'Are you okay?' again for the rest of her life, it would be too soon. Slowly she had shut down: stopped doing anything, stopped saying anything, stopped living. But now the words that had been held inside were starting to come out.

"I'm sick and fucking tired of people asking me if I'm okay! I hate people. I hate this world and all a sudden, thanks to you, I'm a fucking mermaid. Which, of course, is just wonderful, because now I have to deal with a whole new set of assholes."

Finn absorbed what she said but he made no reply, as if he weren't really listening at all. She felt as if she had broken open. It was his fault; everything she had held inside for two years was pouring out into the sand. She stared at him but he wasn't looking at her. He was staring off into the distance just as she had.

"You know what the really fucked up thing is? You're the first one I told. Parents sent me to shrink after shrink, but no, you annoyed me so much that I finally broke. Congratulations on being the biggest dick in the world." He watched as her chest rose and fell as she tried to suppress her sobs. She was angry with herself for everything: for telling, for realizing just how many new problems she had added to her old ones, for remembering.

Finn didn't make a move toward her; instead, he rolled away from her, ignoring her, ignoring her pain. She'd probably leave now, anyway, he hoped. He listened to suppressed sobs until she left, leaving him alone, the way he liked it, the way it should be. He couldn't deny the fact that he was just as dangerous as the horrors that haunted her nightmares. He knew exactly what those nightmares were, only in his nightmares, he was the monster.

Alice made the long swim back to shore. She wasn't thinking of anything. Her head was completely blank, for once, and she was completely numb. The lack of pants became an issue when she hit shore, but she found an old towel on the beach and tied it around her waist. She didn't want anyone to notice her on her way home, dark though it was. She finally landed in her bed at 5:00 am. This time David was in bed already, so she didn't have to worry about spying brothers.

That night, Alice slept. For the first time in two years there were no dreams, no new horrors, just smooth, blissful sleep.

Chapter 9

Changes

"Are you sure we aren't just seeing things that aren't there?" Sarah asked, sitting up in bed, the dark around them. The plans had been made to send Alice away at the beginning of the month, yet they had been duly cancelled. Ron saw in his daughter that he hadn't seen in a long time. Just a way she looked at him, maybe, but it was enough to give the two hope.

Ron rolled over to face his wife. "Something's different," he said assuredly.

"She's the same person, though. She avoids people like she always does. It's just routine." Sarah looked at him, tears shining in her eyes. She had just woken from a nightmare.

"Give her time."

"We've given her an extra month."

"Come here." Ron pulled his wife into his arms. Patting her short hair, he whispered soothing words, though he wasn't at all sure about things himself. The truth was, he wasn't sure they weren't imagining things any more than Sarah was. Still, he felt it in his bones something was different; though Alice looked like the same shell of a person she had been for so long, there were storms in her eyes.

Alice had found a comfortable routine. Things weren't perfect, but her nights weren't plagued by nightmares anymore. Alice found herself avoiding people the way she always did, but for once she could breathe again. Things were quiet, the way she liked them. She fought herself on the inside; while part of her just wanted to let go and give up, the other half of her was stirring inside.

She found herself dreaming again, but it felt more like a memory than a dream.

It was a chilly night in L.A. She and her grandmother were walking from a show to the car. It was quiet and they were alone, but the dark wasn't on their minds then. They were actually laughing. Alice's pregnancy was beginning to show and, with her grandmother's help, she was becoming okay with it. After all, Greg was in prison now, and Alice was far away from the lot of them. Alice had just turned twenty-one, the ocean was nearby and her grandmother understood and loved her; life was taking a turn for the better. It had been Grandma's idea for Alice to take self-defense, but now Alice had grown to love it. She felt stronger than she had in a long time.

That's when the shadow crossed their path. It happened so fast, the argument didn't even register in Alice's brain.

Emma grabbed her chest, she was wheezing, and Alice didn't care there was someone there robbing them: all that mattered was her grandmother. He leapt forward, there was a knife, and she screamed as lightning hit her side, entering her abdomen like it was the consistency of butter. She tried to fight, tried to move, but the pain was so intense, the baby might be hurt, and there her grandmother was. The struggle was all there was. Her head pounded, her body ached, and she was falling to the ground.

The man stood over her, blinking, Alice didn't have the strength to get up, and she smelled blood thick in her nostrils. She turned her head to the side, her eyes thick with tears, and there her grandmother was. She had collapsed. Alice couldn't tell if she was breathing or not.

His hands were all over her, searching her, pulling the wallet from her thin jacket. He pulled the necklace from her grandmother's throat, the one she never took off. His knee grazed Alice's wound and she screamed. He stood up, looked straight at her, and ran, leaving an immobile Alice next to her dying grandmother.

She cried and screamed until her throat was raw, but no one came. It was so late at night: there was no one there. Her loss of blood was too slow for her to pass out, and she lay there crying until finally someone appeared, four hours later. By the time her Good Samaritan showed up, Alice was just beginning to lose consciousness. She had made peace with slipping into the dark night, knowing that her grandmother would never get up again and her daughter would never be born. It had been within the first hour that she saw her grandmother's eyes grow dark. Hope was dead, her grandmother was dead, and no one was coming. But they did, one man came, and when she opened her eyes she was on a gurney being wheeled into an ambulance. They didn't know who she was: her wallet and identification was gone, and there was none on her grandmother, either.

Blood was all they knew: she needed blood. She was unconscious before she got to the hospital. When she woke up again, her parents were there, but nothing was the same.

She woke up screaming, her sheets soaked in sweat.

Everything had been going her way. She was on the swim team and had already won a couple gold medals at competition. She was beautiful, as chic as Finn's fan club. She was everything she had ever wanted to be. She had a great family, great friends, everything going for her. It had all disappeared so quickly. Then, when she had nothing else to give, they took her voice.

She leapt out of the sweat and ran to the bathroom, pushing her mom out of the way in her pursuit for the toilet. The door was wide open as her mother watched her throw up, sadness in her eyes. Alice felt those eyes on her, felt the weight of her mother's judgment. Her mother knew she had been drinking the night before. Alice slammed the door in her mother's face, then returned to the toilet. She burst into tears before she could stop them; she turned away from the toilet and instead put her head to the cool floor. Weeping yet again, remembering the way Finn had just sat there as if her pain was nothing. Everything was nothing, nothing mattered; you couldn't stop the world from tearing you down. Then there was the doctor in her head, and his smile. She threw up again. It was in her hair and around her face, chunks of nothingness that smelled of bile. She gagged in disgust.

Jumping into a cold shower, she let the water wash over her as she leaned against the wall, trying to stop herself from throwing up again. To her, the water just went on and on. It didn't truly feel cold to her skin: she didn't even have the ability to have a cold shower anymore. Hot tears mixed with the cascading ice water. She fell to her knees, letting it wash over her, on and on. Shut out the sounds, shut out the smells, shut out the light, breathe. Shut out the sounds, shut out the smells, shut out the light, breathe. She shook her head, sending drops of water in all directions. It wasn't working, it wasn't working at all. Pushing her forehead into the bottom of the tub, she forced herself to just breathe as her heart pounded in her chest and her hands shook.

After a while, her sobs calmed, and she turned the water off. Slowly, she moved to her feet and crawled out of the tub. Lethargically, she moved to the mirror to mechanically brush her teeth—then she stopped. She looked at her reflection in the mirror.

Her hair was so long that it was flat, and horribly tangled. It had none of the bounce it had when she had it shoulder-length. It simply hung, obscuring her bright green eyes and her gorgeous cheekbones. Her clothes hid the hourglass form hidden underneath. They also shrouded the scar from the knife; the faint stretch marks would disappear within the year. Her skin was pale like death, but a few days out in that sun and she might even have some life in her skin. She was suddenly seeing herself the way everyone else did, and she didn't recognize herself. She tried to run her fingers through her hair but instantly got caught in knots.

She was still there, somewhere, underneath all her layers of protection. She knew it, she could see. Her eyes still shone through the entire mess she had made of herself, the mess that was created out of the girl she had been. Through screams and trauma, Alice was still there. For the first time in years, Alice was looking at herself, and she was puzzled. She wasn't the same girl anymore. She could never go back to being that happy girl, to living the college life with her Joss Whedon-obsessed roommate, to late night jokes and study halls and concerts. She couldn't be that girl anymore; the girl that her mother wanted.

So who exactly was she?

She saw the ocean in her mirror, teeming with life, and she relaxed. She looked at her hands as a spark traveled from one finger to the other. She was a living stun gun. Looking down at herself, she tentatively touched her scar. She wasn't the same; she was something else. She was mer, she was a woman, and she had survived. Alice surfaced for just a moment, taking a deep breath for the first time in years. A knock on the door interrupted her reverie.

"Honey, are you okay in there?" Her mother asked, her voice worried with a tint of frustration and fear, fear that she had lost her daughter forever. Behind the fear, though, Alice heard a note of hope.

"I'll be out in a minute," Alice said.

"Honey, could you come downstairs when you're done? Your father and I need to talk to you."

Instantly Alice was alarmed. Her father should be at work, exactly where she'd be heading at one o'clock. She left the bathroom and looked at the clock. It was already seven a.m. Dad should definitely be at work. She slowly crept down the stairs in her towel and bathrobe. Mom was sitting at one end of the table with Dad's hands on her shoulders. He was dressed for work. Alice tentatively lowered herself into the chair across from them.

"Honey, this has to stop. Your mother and I just can't do this anymore."

"You're always in the bar. You're never home."

"And you keep showing up at God-awful hours in the morning."

"We just can't handle you drinking yourself to death," her mother said sadly, staring at Alice, pleading with her to hear the voice of reason. Pleading with Alice to just come back from the edge she thought Alice was so ready to jump from.

"We've been mulling over this decision for a long time, and we thought we'd tell you: if you don't change, we are going to have to send you away."

Alice stared at them and saw their faces in a new light. Her mother looked away, surprised at Alice's gaze, but Alice could tell that her mother was biting her lip. For the first time in a long time, Alice could see how much her parents hurt for her. They knew there was nothing they could do, but they couldn't handle it any more than she had been able to, handle that feeling of impotency. They had been hurt because she was hurt, because her pain had torn apart the family, because they had suffered loss, too. Her father had lost his mother, both of them had lost their daughter and granddaughter, and their son was nearly as bad, preferring to spend time with his machines instead of another human being. Her family had fallen apart because of her, because of the violence that had touched her. Alice was there, she was sitting with her family and seeing their pain, but not touching it, not yet. First she had to touch herself; it was her apathy that was the root of the problem.

"I've been swimming, late at night." It was the truth. She said it in the dead voice she knew so well, and it sickened her, hearing that tone in her voice.

"All alone?" Sarah paused, "At night?" For once, Alice didn't fail to recognize the tinge of worry to her voice. She looked up at her mother as Ron shot Sarah a look that said, *She's okay. At least she's doing something.* Sarah stopped and stared at her daughter with wonder. They knew she could swim and they were worried about her going out alone, but what could they do? She was an adult, after all.

"I-I think I'm going to get a haircut today," Alice said slowly, remembering the way her fingers stuck in the tangles and the flat, dead way it hung against her skin. Her parents just stared at her: they could hardly believe she'd responded to them at all, and they knew what it meant for Alice to cut her hair. Sarah shot a hopeful look at her husband, unshed tears swimming in her eyes. Sarah didn't know it, but her faint spark of hope finally became a flame at that moment. Ron's face said, *I don't know. I just don't know.*

Alice got up, leaving her parents there, and went upstairs to put on some clothes. She would go to the barber, maybe the clothes shop before work if she could swing it in time. She didn't want to be the person she saw reflected in the mirror. She wanted part of herself back; the first step would be to come out of the costumes she used to hide herself. The hair, the clothing, the blank stare; she needed to show herself in order to become herself again. After all, she wasn't as weak as she was before. Reflexively, she let the electricity run along her fingers.

She logged on to David's computer and was surprised how easy it was to find an old picture of the two of them. The first ones she found were from one of the times when she came back from college one semester. It was on one of those rare sunny days in Oregon. They were in Pioneer Square, hanging onto a statue, a man with an umbrella. There were other photos, too, but that was all she needed. Printing one off, she heard the door slam as her father left for work. She went downstairs and passed her mom, who watched her from her position at the kitchen counter. Alice ignored her mom's stares, grabbed her purse and headed to the local barber.

She walked in and up to the counter. The shop had just opened and there was no one else in there.

"I need a haircut. Can you squeeze me in now?" Alice asked.

The woman at the counter looked up, "Yes, you do." she said, looking at Alice's hair rather than her face. Alice tried a smile. It was so rusty it came out completely distorted, and she was sure she probably looked more scary than happy to the woman. The woman turned away awkwardly. Next thing she knew, she was in the chair with the cape wrapped around her.

The stylist was staring at Alice's reflection in the mirror, handling her hair with distaste. Alice was sure that her hair was probably the stylist's worst nightmare come to life.

"I don't think I could wash all this in our little sinks, so we're gonna cut some and then wash it, if that's okay, unless you just want a trim." It was clear that a trim wasn't actually an option.

Alice pulled the picture from her purse. "I want this back," she said, pointing to her shoulder-length 'do.

"Cute kid. Is that your brother?" The stylist brightened slightly.

"Yeah."

"What's that statue?"

"Just some random statue in Portland."

"You sure you wanna lose that much? I mean, I could cut it up to the middle of your back if you wanted…" The stylist stared at Alice's hair, not sure at all if she could perform even that small miracle. It was like looking at the destruction a tornado had performed on a house and having to figure out what to fix first.

Alice looked at her frumpy self in the mirror again. She was going to change, she was resigned to it. Her grandmother wouldn't have approved of the mess she had become. It was time Alice came out of the clouds. "Yes, I'm sure."

Alice walked to work as usual, but this time she had just finished shopping and she was carrying a few bags full of clothes.

"Hey, Alice! Nice 'do," Ted said as she walked in. Alice forced another awkward smile. The smiling thing was hard to get used to again.

"Do you mind if I change into some of my new clothes before work?" Alice asked awkwardly.

"Something not frumpy?" Ted said hopefully. He hadn't really agreed with Alice's choice of clothes, but hadn't dared talk to her before. She was an okay worker, but her attitude was subpar. She was supposed to be a salesperson, not a zombie in the corner. He had given her the job at the request of her father, who he was seeing for massive dental work. The only reason he said something was that her forced smile and new hair-cut had made him daring. Her hair did look great. It looked like honey, lit by the sunshine. It had body, it framed her pale cheekbones. There was more mist than cloud in her eyes and the bright green definitely shined.

"Something not frumpy," Alice affirmed. Ted nodded.

Alice emerged from the dressing room in a mostly green halter and form-fitting jeans. Ted spit coffee all over his books.

"What do you think?" Alice asked tentatively, not sure what his reaction meant anymore. Ted couldn't believe it. This frumpy girl who had been working for him for a few months was a model in disguise. She spun around. Ted was her dad's age. He was friendly with everyone but didn't scare Alice one bit. He was heavyset and happily married; at least, happily married for the second time.

"Your, uh, tag is still on the halter." Ted said. "Let me get that for you." He grabbed the scissors, approaching her slowly. Alice flinched slightly when he cut the tag from her, but she knew he was just trying to help.

The rest of the day passed uneventfully until around three.

Ted looked up from the books he did in between customers. She was hanging new swim suits on the rack and he was looking out the window.

"Here comes one of the strange girls," he nodded. Alice looked up. All her awkwardness about her new-old look suddenly disappeared as Kari, distracted by Alice's new look, ran straight into the shop's glass door. Alice laughed without meaning to at little Kari face-planting herself into the glass with that gaped mouth look on her face. It was impossible not to laugh; except, apparently, for Ted, who jumped when he heard Alice laugh.

If her parents had been there, if her brother had been there, they would have stared in disbelief. This wasn't an awkward smile, this wasn't a forced laugh; this was mirth, true and real, something they hadn't heard from her since before her unfortunate history. For years her family hadn't heard a laugh like that. After his initial reaction of surprise, all Ted could do was smile. He thought it was strange that he didn't remember her ever laughing before.

Kari picked herself up, not hiding the fact she was openly staring at Alice through the glass. After a moment of disbelief, Kari ran at top speed toward the ocean.

Alice was wiping tears of laughter out of her eyes. "Why do you call them strange, Ted?"

"They're always buying swimsuits, but not a whole swimsuit, no, not those girls. They only buy tops. God only knows what they're doing with themselves." Ted sounded disgusted, Alice

113

suppressed another laugh. She knew exactly why they didn't buy bottoms. She had definitely shredded enough clothing to know exactly what would happen to a swimsuit bottom on a girl who grew a tail after jumping in the water.

Alice was okay. Well certainly far from okay, but she was herself, she noticed people. She was there. She wasn't just a wall that people occasionally addressed. As she left work, she looked at the ocean and smiled faintly. *Not tonight,* she thought. Tonight Alice headed home. She didn't know why, she just knew that right then it was where she should be.

She got home a little after seven. Her family looked up from dinner. There was a spot set out for her, but she had never used it before. Her parents couldn't believe what they were seeing as she stepped through the door. David looked up from his meal, eager to return to his games but froze.

It was as if he was seeing a ghost, his sister, it was her again, but the look in her eyes belonged to someone else. He stared at her up and down looking at her, looking at the person she was combined with whatever she was now. After a moment of staring at each other, David pushed his chair back and came toward her. For a tense moment he just studied her closer, and she looked back at him, into his sad eyes. In one sharp instant, his arms were around her.

"I love you, Aly," he said. After freezing stiff for a

moment, unsure of how to respond, she wrapped her arms around her little brother. In his embrace she felt as calm as she did in the water. It was a small step, but it was a step all the same, and a big one for Alice. No one had been able to touch Alice in a long time. Alice smiled a real smile.

Chapter 10

A Fish A Day

October began, refreshing breezes blew off the water, and everyone was out on the beach. The water was absolutely perfect in the rising temperatures. Alice was never herself more than when she was alone and swimming through the wonders of the blue. She liked to swim with one whale in particular; it sang to her, told her of wonders she hadn't explored. The mer world touched her occasionally, but, for the most part, she kept to herself. It was becoming harder to avoid their world when she knew so little about it.

This was how she found herself on a mission after work one day. She had a destination in mind, so she single-mindedly set out for it. She walked straight into the clinic.

"Is Adam in?" She asked the receptionist, idly noticing the gaudy nameplate that said Natalie.

"Yes; he's just stitching a cut on a boy's leg." Alice moved to go in through the back door. "But you can't go in there!" Natalie called after her. Alice didn't notice; she certainly wasn't listening. She walked past one of the rooms, lucky that the door was open. Inside, Adam was carefully lecturing a young boy.

"Let's try not to do any more dangerous stunts, Johnny. You

could've broken a leg." Johnny, clearly not paying much attention, looked past Adam and smiled, a sucker perched precariously in his mouth. Adam, confused, turned to follow the little boy's gaze.

"Alice!" He yelped in surprise. It was a good thing he had been done stitching: he hadn't seen Alice since her haircut and shopping spree. At that point, Natalie caught up to them, out of breath; she must have been at least thirty years older than Adam.

"I'm sorry, she just barged in. I couldn't stop her."

"It's okay, Natalie. Alice is a friend. Would you mind taking Johnny back out to his parents?" Natalie agreed and began to usher the boy out.

"Alice…what are you doing here?" Adam asked as Natalie turned to leave. He knew a pretty girl had hidden under all that hair and clothes, but to see her in person blew him away. It was a drastic change.

"I want to know more," she demanded. They both knew the office wasn't a good place to talk, so Adam invited her to walk with him.

"What do you want to know?" he asked as they started down the sidewalk. It made him slightly uncomfortable to stand next to the person she was now. The change in her was palpable.

"Anything you do. Finn's posse talked about mating. What's the deal with that?"

"Honestly, it's like an animal in heat..." Adam said

awkwardly, looking Alice up and down out of the corner of his eye. "I mean they just, it's just...I don't know how to describe it," he rubbed some of the building sweat off his brow. "The folk mate for life, and somehow they know."

"Know what?"

"Well, you know the old sayings about kissing a ton of frogs before you find the right one? Well with the folk, you know the instant your lips connect that you're destined to be."

"How is that even possible? I mean, with all the people divorcing these days…"

"Yeah, humans divorcing, sure. But, like I was trying to say, with the folk, they know. Something about the electrical current, I think. I really have no idea. You guys won't really let me study you, after all."

"How would one mate with a human, then?"

"You know, a human has a low current, too." He paused, sighing with frustration. "I honestly don't know. Half of what the folk are is pure magic to me, because my science can't grasp it."

"So now you're calling me magic?"

Adam stopped and looked at her. He wasn't quite sure if she was joking; he couldn't read the tone in her voice. She just stared back at him with no hint of what she really meant. He shook it off and just continued.

"Somewhere between winter and spring, I guess, is the peak

for mating, but I don't know much about the social aspects. I mean, certain members of the folk I'd know...You're really talking to the wrong person," he scratched his head. She was confusing the issue with the way she was looking at him; she seemed so different from the woman he had seen so often in the bar. "All I really do is treat the wounds from your fights."

"Knife fights?"

"Yeah, territorial, female or male disputes, they're all settled by your weapons. That's why it was so important you had one. Where is yours, anyway?" he said, trying to change the topic.

"Under my pillow."

"You should find a better place for it." They were continuing their walk, and it was all Adam could do not to just stop and stare at her. Why were all the folk so gorgeous, anyway?

"Why are all the women chasing Finn? He's an asshole. I don't care if his grandmother is dying." Adam stopped in his tracks. That was one way to get his attention.

"How do you know that?"

"How do you?" Alice countered.

"I treat her."

"He told me."

"Finn told you about his grandmother? Brassila?" Finn didn't talk to anyone about anything, let alone someone who was completely new to their clan.

"Brassila?" Alice's eyes widened with surprise.

"Yes."

"I didn't know." Alice said, shocked. Brassila had just been a story that a guy in a bar told her. She hadn't really applied Adam's story to what was happening to her now. Adam shook his head, clearing some line of thought he wasn't going to discuss.

"The girls chase him because he's a prize: the mansion will go to him, which means he has a safe landfall. He also has a lot of human wealth and power. And because he's waited far longer than usual to choose a mate."

"How old is he?"

"Around 26. His brother's about 18: this is Tommy's first mating season."

"They don't pair before?"

"Well, I know they kiss people, maybe experiment some, but they can't feel that spark before 18." He eyed her suspiciously, "You're not planning on going after Finn, are you?"

She looked shocked. "Me? Finn? No offense, but he's a pampered brat. Besides I don't need anybody." He stepped away from her as he watched a spark reflexively travel across two of her fingers. "No man gets that close to me," she said, slipping back into her old clouds briefly. It had a different effect when she was all cleaned and primped like one of the other maids. He watched the current travel across her fingers again: she was dangerous but beautiful, but she was also one of them. Somehow he just couldn't get his mind on one track.

"Please, don't do that near me. It was bad enough when you were drunk; I don't want to know how bad it is sober." Alice turned to him, seeing an odd fear in his eyes. For a moment they stood there, looking at each other, before they both burst into mild laughter. Alice looked around as she recovered: they were at his doorstep. She hadn't even noticed which direction they had been going..

"Why do you care if I go after Finn anyway?"

"I have a feeling some of those maids think Finn is their territory. They'd defend it with their knives. Which is why you should always keep yours on you. Your haircut could be enough to set them off, let alone...the rest," he said, pausing and looking away. At the mention of knives, Alice's hand instinctively went to her scar. Adam noticed but said nothing. "You, uh...wanna come in for dinner?" Adam asked awkwardly. She looked up. Was he asking her on a date? She couldn't be sure, and she certainly didn't trust the doctor who was paid to deal with her kind. Adam didn't even know why he was asking her; he certainly didn't want to get involved with the mer, it just seemed like the courteous thing to do.

"No, I should go home," she said after a pause. "My family, they just, they need me right now. I'll see you later. If I have more questions."

"You know, there're people in the underwater city like Misa

who will answer your questions. Not to mention she would know way more than I could ever tell you." Alice froze for a moment, then continued on her way. She didn't tell him that she wanted nothing to do with either humans or merfolk, that she wanted little more than being left alone. Just because she had changed her appearance didn't mean she wasn't still the scared and traumatized woman inside.

Alice looked better, but it was for herself, and her family's benefit. It was a start, but it wasn't the solution. Alice didn't want anyone else. The only reason she was curious about the merfolk was because she figured she should probably know more if she was going to survive. The only thing she cared about was the ocean, and her family. Her family hurt for her, hurt with her, hurt because of her, and needed her to put back together what she had torn apart. She walked home that night and ate dinner with her family. Eating with her family was a singular act that did nothing but bring smiles to her parent's faces, and that was reward enough. She had put them through enough suffering.

Chapter 11

Snowless Christmas

"This is stupid, Dad," David said, hanging an ornament on the artificial tree as Alice looked for music on the radio and her parents attempted to take pictures. It was December now, and David was out of school. It was a little late for their tradition of putting up the tree, but the season had crept up on them. The holiday was different when occurring amidst the heat, grilling on the barbies.

"This isn't Christmas-like at all! I mean, there's no snow...there's not even rain! Or clouds. It's sunny and hot outside!" David continued.

"I think it's a great Christmas: no shoveling and I can still go swimming," Alice said. Truthfully, it was much more difficult to go swimming, considering the beaches were growing a little crowded.

"You two are ridiculous. It never snowed in Portland for Christmas." Sarah put in while trying to get a picture of the two kids together.

"Welcome to the tropics, kids," Ron said coming in from getting the mail. Alice returned to helping David with the ornaments. "Hey, Aly, you have something here."

"What?"

"Looks like an invitation of some sort." Her mom walked over first.

"The Caraway mansion! When did you meet the Caraway boys?" her mother asked.

"Finn?" Alice stepped over the boxes full of Christmas decorations in their cramped living room. With both parents looking over her shoulder, she opened the invitation.

"It's addressed to you and a guest," her mother said. She eyed Alice, looking for some reaction. Alice didn't always react, but she figured her daughter might have told her she had met one of the Caraways.

"Live band...wow," said her father.

"It's just a Christmas party," Alice shrugged.

"A Christmas party, at a mansion, on a private beach," her mother's eyes looked misty.

"That's not fair!" David said. "Why Aly and not us?"

"I dunno, must be really exclusive," Ron replied.

"They probably want a younger crowd," said Sarah, sounding mildly disappointed. "I mean, the Caraways are pretty young, and they have a huge mansion all to themselves." Alice choked down a grunt before it came out. The Caraways were rarely alone. With their private beach and large mansion, they frequently housed several members of the mer community whenever they chose to stay on land overnight.

"I'm young!" David said.

"How'd you meet the Caraways?" Ron asked curiously, ignoring David.

"We've run into each other once or twice. I didn't think much of it."

"Apparently they did," her mother said. Alice wasn't about to tell them that it was probably a party where he invited the local merfolk. Because then they'd have a conversation something to the tune of: *so, mom, who in our history was a mermaid? Because somehow I'm one, too.*

"Our daughter, friends with a millionaire!" her dad said, patting Alice on the back. She didn't say that "friend" was probably the last thing she would call either Finn or Tommy.

"I probably won't even go. It's in a week…right on Christmas day? I should probably spend that night with you."

"Oh, no you don't, honey. You don't get invited to a fancy formal dress party by a millionaire and not go. I'll even buy you a dress! You don't have anything formal enough for a mansion." Alice rolled her eyes at her mother's obvious excitement.

"Please, Mom, don't buy my dress."

"Honey! There's nowhere in town to get a fancy dress. You'd have to go to the city."

"If, and I mean *if* I'm going, I'll figure out a way to get to town, mother. Anyway, I have to go. I told Adam I'd go sailing with him today," she said, throwing the invitation at the kitchen counter. Her mother smiled at Ron knowingly. Alice had been spending a fair amount of time sailing with Adam. Of course, Alice wasn't necessarily always spending that time with Adam, but it was a good excuse when she went on long swimming excursions.

"What about the ornaments?" David cried.

"I thought we were done, little brother?"

"I guess we are," he said grudgingly.

"I'll catch you all later."

Alice all but ran down the road. She couldn't wait. The water this time of year felt great. No one was down on the beach just now. There were some people surfing, but it didn't matter, no one was watching her. As she ran for the shore, she was reminded of her grandma, cheering her on more than anyone at the competitions. She hadn't told her parents the whole truth. When she did meet Adam, she frequently swam to him. Unless, of course, the beach was crowded, then she did bum a ride from him. This time, Adam had left an hour or so ago and was already a couple miles out to sea, but Alice would catch up soon enough.

Alice twirled and danced among the life in the water. It was divine; she could tell why the people were out on surfboards. Perhaps the reason their little beach was so empty was because most people went to nicer beaches. The local beach wasn't that great because the shore was fairly rocky, but it didn't stop everyone. Alice had to be more careful that she wasn't seen in daylight.

Still, the ocean was perfect. The fish and other creatures of the deep were around her and the water was heaven. It didn't take her long to swim out past the surfers toward a boat. She knew it was Adam's, so she wasn't afraid. She arced out of the water, making sure to splash the captain in his summer turtleneck. Alice was wearing her green bikini top. She bobbed to the surface.

"I knew it was you. More questions?" he asked.

"Just one," she yelled up.

"Which means somewhere around ten. You coming up?"

Alice thought about it a moment. It would be easier than screaming up at him, though she didn't really want to leave the water. "If you've got a towel and some pants."

"I might have something around here somewhere, it's not like I do this all the time now or anything." He smiled. His smile still unnerved her, but less than before. She and Adam had developed a tentative friendship over the past couple of months. She was trying very hard to be human again, and Adam was trying to get over the fact that she wasn't human. It wasn't an ideal situation, but it was sort of working, for now.

Minutes later, Alice found herself on deck. The towel was draped over her shoulders and she wore an old pair of Adam's sweatpants, with a hole in one knee. He quickly offered her a beer and she took it. It was hard for him to be around her without something to do.

"So, what question you got for me?" Adam asked. He lounged back in the booth, watching her carefully. He felt if he played things too quickly, she would slip through his fingers like an eel, but the soft smiles that lit up her green eyes were something he lived for.

"Could my family be transforms?"

He stared at her, "Why would you ask that?"

"I'm just curious."

"Your brother probably is, and one of your parents probably carries the gene. But how could you even think of that?"

"Could I ever tell any of them about this?" She said gesturing at the ocean, the stupid smile that she always carried after swimming painted on her face, the one that lit her green eyes the way nothing else did.

"What? Hanging out on a boat belonging to the local doctor without your own pants? Swimming two miles in the ocean, without taking a breath, mind you, to intercept my boat? I knew you weren't only going to ask one question." He tried to play it off sarcastically, but part of him liked that he could share this with her. Even though she was a mer now, once upon a time she had been human. He liked to flatter himself that this was why she came to him.

"You know what I mean," she said frowning.

He lost the sarcastic smile on his own face. "No, you can't tell them. Not unless you got approval from a clan leader."

"A clan leader? We have clan leaders now?"

"Of course you do,"

"Why did I not know this?"

"You never seemed interested in their politics before, and you do seem pretty adept at avoiding them...especially your suitors..." he stifled a laugh; she frowned in his general direction.

"Who   are   the   leaders?"
"Who do you think, genius?"

"Finn. Finn's the leader."

"No, his grandmother is. But when she does finally pass, he will be the next clan leader."

"So I'm supposed to ask Mr.-smarty-pants-stay-off-my-island jerk?"

"Stop, stop, stop. Let's just back up a second. What are you looking for? Hasn't your family suffered enough without knowing all this? I mean, do you know the consequences of what you're asking?"

She stared at him in response, waiting for him to tell her.

"Alice, this is your burden to carry, you can't..."

"I can't bring my brother into this? I can never really get close to my family again? I can't ever have the sibling I remember?"

Adam sighed. "I didn't say that, it's just... Alice...the consequence *if* Brassila did say yes, and that's a big if, mind you..."

"So I can't go to the asshole."

"Until Brassila dies it has to be her." He looked off at the ocean, "Wits are something she hasn't lost."

"Alice," he turned back to her, took her hands in his. She flinched but accepted it. She had been getting better at that, and better at not shocking him every time he did it. "You'd be risking his life. If it turned out your brother didn't have the gene... he would be killed. They can't have someone knowing their secrets. As for your parents, it's likely one of them is and one is not a recessive mer. There's really no way to tell. Either way, if you share the secret to someone who cannot become a mer, they will not live." She looked straight at him with those clear green eyes and he found it hard to return her gaze. He couldn't be sure she understood what he was saying.

"My brother."

He released her hands gently. "Could you live with his blood on your hands?"

She looked off into the distance, at the ocean, and he

watched that faded smile crawl across her face. She was beneath those waves again in her head. It irritated him a little that she had a place he couldn't follow.

"You can't know what's down there."

"Your father said you two were very close." Her smile brightened just a little.

"I miss him. I feel like I'm lying to him every day when I go home."

"But,"

"I could never. I want to share this all with him," she turned back to Adam, "You can't begin to imagine." He sighed. When she talked like that, she was one of them.

"Alice," he reached for her again. This time she jerked away.

"What about this party?" she asked. He sighed. He was used to this; sometimes she would be on one topic and then suddenly another. When she got too deep into something emotionally, she would quickly turn tail and disappear into her mind to finish her arguments with herself, and by herself. He watched as she let the current reflexively run across her fingers. She liked to do that when she got lost in her head.

"You can't get out of the fish party, I'm afraid. You're the transform, so you are number one on the priority list. They will miss you if you are not there."

"Well, do you wanna go?" she asked casually. At this casual, benign question though, he froze.

"To the Caraway Christmas party?"

"Are you even allowed?" she wondered.

"Well, yes, but I'd probably be the only humans there," he looked thoughtful, than mumbled something else, "and I'd have to take certain precautions."

"I meant as a friend, Adam. You're the only person I know, the only person in the town I could remotely call a friend. I think it would be as awkward going with a human as it would be going alone. In this case, I don't really want to be alone."

"No, you wouldn't want to do that, being single and of age…" He nodded deep in thought. It would probably calm Ashley down a bit; even if he were only a friend, the sharks didn't have to know that. Not to mention it would balk any suitors. He knew, even as a friend, that the last thing she needed was someone who didn't understand what she was going through. Also, he had seen Ashley lately for a cut she received from one of the visiting mer. Which reminded him: "Hey, where's your knife?"

"Oh, I must have left it at home."

"How many times have I told you?"

"I don't think those witches care about me. I haven't moved for their territory."

"You don't have any idea!"

"What?"

"Ashley's chomping at the bit."

"You been talking to your buddy Finn?"

"Go home, Alice, and don't come to the party without that knife. I'll rent a tux. Do you have a dress?"

"No. Actually, I was wondering if you could drive me into the city to look for one."

He smiled. "You're asking a guy to go shopping with you?"

"Not like I know anyone else. We only have one car and my parents will be using it."

"Your mom would kill to go shopping with you." The look of horror on Alice's face made him laugh. "Too traumatic, huh? Yeah, I'll be your lift. I'll pick you up a little after five tomorrow. As far as the party goes, I'll pick you up six o'clock Christmas day. In my car, not my boat." He smiled.

"Ooh, driving a car in Brassila Cove, must be fancy." Alice finished her beer, got up and gracefully wrapped her towel around her just before she let the sweatpants fall to the ground. She walked off the deck and threw the wet towel back up to Adam. "Sorry 'bout your towel!" He caught it and shook his head at her. Everything with her was quick: get in, get out, spend as little time in the company of others as possible. Yet, still, she had convinced her parents that she was moving forward in leaps and bounds. Adam could tell different. The more time she spent in the water, the more she moved further and further away from every sentient creature around her. In a world that large, it wasn't hard.

Alice went home and up to her room; it was getting late now. Her parents were in bed, but David was wide awake, sitting at his computer per usual. He was probably the only other person who didn't think Alice had really improved that much. David had been fooled briefly when she cut her hair, but the way she avoided him told him something completely different. Alice walked past him to enter her room. She flopped on the bed, her hand instinctively reaching up under the pillow for her knife, grasping onto thin air. Alice froze. She all but jumped up and walked the few steps to David's room.

David spun in the chair at his desk as she fell against his door frame. In his hands was her knife. She stared at his accusatory eyes in disbelief. It wasn't something one would expect to find in a young woman's room. The curve of the blade looked deadly.

"David..." she whispered, unable to really get any breath behind it.

"Alice, what is this?" he asked.

"You haven't told mom or dad, have you?" Alice's heart was tight in her chest. The knife. Any answer she could give would lead to more questions. More questions that would lead straight to a secret that could be deadly for her family. He wasn't supposed to know. She wasn't supposed to have to make this decision; she understood what Adam had tried to tell her. The folk never took their rules, or their secrecy, lightly.

"No," he answered, softly. Alice let out a breath of relief. At least he hadn't involved their parents. She knew her parents would question it relentlessly. The knife was encrusted with shells that weren't easily found in diving distance. David knew that, and Alice knew he knew, he was an internet whiz, he would have looked them up, taken pictures, referenced them. This was information he would gladly share with his less internet savvy parents. She stared into his eyes and she melted.

"It's, I-I'm sorry, David, it's a secret I have to keep." She couldn't even bring herself to make up some lie for him, despite them being distant for so long. "I promise I'll tell you when you're older."

"I turn 18 on January second, Alice."

"Right. I'll tell you when you're an adult. I promise." He handed the knife back to her.

"You had better,"

"Just don't tell anyone, or the deal's off." She didn't know how she was possibly going to tell him anything, but she had to say something. If only to keep it a secret for awhile. *Great,* she thought as she curled up in bed, the knife back where it belonged. *Now I have to talk to Finn. No not Finn, Finn's grandmother.* She slipped into uneasy sleep, with visions of the deep dancing through her head.

Chapter 12

Men and Shopping

"How about this one?" Alice asked. Adam raised his head from his hands. He couldn't fathom how he had ever agreed to this. Spending time with Alice was one thing, but spending time with a woman shopping was just not something a male was biologically adapted to. The long drive there had been mostly silent; he had had to turn the radio on just to maintain his sanity. Now he watched her try on dress after terrible dress. They were either so fluffy they hid everything, or too long, or just ugly things made of material akin to burlap.

"Alice, how 'bout I pick the next few?" he asked tentatively but desperately. She flinched in response. "No offense, Alice, it's just...you're not thinking fancy, you're thinking...well, I don't know what you're thinking, but whatever it is, it's terrible." She just stared at him. They had been at it at least an hour and neither had eaten. She was getting tired of being told everything was wrong. Even the sales clerks were giving her weird looks. She admitted to herself that she *was* fashion-challenged at that point; she was terrified of this silly little ball. Pants were one thing, but a dress meant something completely different.

She went back into the changing room with a frown on her

face. Adam went to the racks and started grabbing some dresses that looked a little better than what she had been picking.

"Wait," she said, coming from behind him to put one of his selections back on the rack.

"Seriously, Alice, we're getting nowhere with what you're picking."

"I know, it's just..." she bit her lip for a second. "Okay, I'll try these on." She took the bundle from him. As she was walking back to the dressing room she grabbed one more dress on impulse before realizing it was something she would have picked before.

She tried the impulsive choice first. Looking in the mirror, she cringed. It wasn't that the dress was terrible; it actually looked great on her. But whether she could wear it in front of anyone was another question. She had it off before she knew it, trying on one of Adam's picks next.

"How's this one?" she asked, coming out of the dressing room. Adam looked up with his same sulky face, then paused midair.

"Not bad, actually," he said as she turned. The black, tea-length gown had a halter top with a keyhole. It was elegant and tasteful, but her form was painfully visible. "It looks fine. Can we be done now?" Alice asked as she retreated back into the dressing room and put her own clothes. Though the black dress was exactly what she had been looking for, she grabbed her impulse choice as well.

Exiting, she smiled her little broken smile, the smile that pulled at his heartstrings. "I'm so hungry!" she exclaimed.

Adam looked thoughtful. "Actually, I know the perfect place," he said as they walked to the checkout counter.

"Oh?" she remarked, feigning interest. As long as she could get some food before she fell over, she was sure it would be fine.

He looked at her out of the corner of his eye. "Well, you will have to change into one of your new dresses," he smiled slyly. He almost laughed at the suspicious look she gave him, but she didn't complain at all.

That was how they landed at Le Petit Crab. The building was mostly glass, and it looked out onto the ocean. Outside, thousands of tiny white lights wound around the bushes and the trees growing from their pots. It was undeniably fancy: not really Alice's idea of food or fun.

"Just call it rehearsal," Adam said to her kindly as she stared at the restaurant. She shot him an angry look as a waiter led them to a table on the balcony overlooking the sea. Still, while she seethed in anger at Adam and tried to make herself comfortable in her halter dress, she couldn't deny that it was beautiful. At the other tables there were some people up and dancing. One elderly couple in particular reminded her of her grandparents, the little she could remember of their forty-year marriage. She had been ten when her grandfather had died, but she had known that when the two were together, they were happy. Alice looked out at the black ocean, her arms across her chest as if she were cold.

"Feel free to order whatever you want: it's on me," Adam said. Alice looked down at the menu. She'd probably just have the crab. She couldn't understand half of what was written on the menu, anyway. She looked out over the ocean again, dreaming, seeing the life that teamed under the surface, wanting, needing. "Hey, what're you thinking about?" Adam asked gently. Alice looked at him distantly. He smiled his winning smile, so she told him the truth.

"My grandmother. She used to look out at the sea after my grandfather died. She'd never go near it, but she always looked like she was waiting for the sea to tell her something. Like all the knowledge in the world could be found beneath the waves."

"She sounds like an amazing woman."

"She was amazing to me. She was always so happy. She cared for the people around her so much more than herself, but when she thought no one was looking, she would get this distant look in her eyes." Adam was sure he knew exactly what that had looked like; Alice could never hide it as well. She snapped out of her reverie and caught him watching her. "I'm sorry," he apologized hastily as she looked away. Afraid to make a connection with anyone, human or mer.

"What happened to her?" he asked seriously. Alice looked up as if he had just stabbed her. He reached out and grabbed her hand. She sent a light shock through it but didn't pull her hand away. The shock wasn't as bad as the first time he had touched her hand; this current was almost pleasant. "Hey, it's okay," he said, forcing himself through the jolt. "I don't mean to pry. It just sounds like you loved her very much." Alice was silent for a moment, just staring into his dark eyes. It made him mildly uncomfortable and aware of the way his hand awkwardly wrapped around hers. It was as if she were piercing him with arrows or darts, like she was shocking him again, though no current ran through her.

"She was murdered." The way Alice said it, he knew. He knew that she was there when her grandmother died. She didn't have to speak it aloud, it was obvious. Now he knew just one more bit of the mystery that was Alice, and he backed off. As he released her stiff, freezing cold hand, she pulled it back in to her lap. For a moment, an awkward silence fell. Luckily, the server showed up shortly thereafter. They ordered, Alice in that dead way she had, staring at the table.

"Well, I'm glad you didn't order lobster." He said a few minutes later, trying to lighten the atmosphere just a little. She looked up at him, confused, "You know, Daryl Hannah, in *Splash*? I was trying to make a joke." Alice laughed a little. It was enough. "Come on."

"Wait, what are you doing?" she asked worriedly as he

pulled her to her feet. "No, Adam, no." But it was too late, it was do or die. If she stopped him, she'd bring attention to them, and attention was the last thing she wanted, so they danced to soft jazz playing over the speakers.

"Come on, you're not that bad," he said, knowing that wasn't the reason she had resisted at all.

She looked at him. She meant to send him a glare of death, but his smile interrupted her. Adam's smile softened something in her; it was so peaceful, and it did feel good to be dancing, like she was moving through the waves of the sea. She let go and let him lead her, letting the music sweep her away. As she danced, soon she was humming. Adam quickly put his hand over her mouth before the entire restaurant turned to look. She looked up at him, confused. He shook his head, breaking the moment.

"Don't- you can't do that. You can't sing like that out of the water," he whispered fiercely. Obviously Alice didn't understand what was going on, so he was forced to explain. "Out of water, that singing is a siren's song. The mer language, sung out of water, attracts way more attention than you want." She looked at him. He sent her into a spin and then pulled her back to him. She was in his arms now, her back against his chest. It was awkward, but it didn't feel wrong and she didn't feel threatened; they were dancing. She wondered about the song for a minute. She knew how special singing was to mer in the water, but it hadn't occurred to her that out of the water it was something completely different. After a few moments, the dancing lulled her and she fell back into the peaceful moment. She closed her eyes again and didn't pull away until their dinner was served. Even then, her mind was somewhere else.

They ate in silence. Alice would never admit that, for a moment, out of the water, life had been okay. The rest of the evening was uneventful. Adam drove her home and she fell asleep in the car. Looking at the way her hair fell over her eyes while her chest rose and fell to the rhythm of the night, Adam didn't want to wake her. The night stretched around them. Life wasn't so horrible. That night something had softened in Alice, and the world turned on its axis in a way that didn't make Alice want to scream.

Chapter 13

Hell of a Party

"That's enough primping, mom! Jeez, you'd think I was on my way to my first homecoming or something!"

"Don't they usually have up-dos at prom?" Ron commented from his position on the couch.

"Show them!" her mom said excitedly. Alice awkwardly tugged at the hem of her dress, the impulsive purchase from a few days before. She had argued with her mom about which one to wear, and her mother thought the midnight blue one looked better for a fancy party than the halter dress. It was gorgeous on her. It was the shortest thing Alice had worn in many years. The spaghetti strap dress was knee-length, low in front and lower in back, with a slit up one side. It made Alice uncomfortable, especially with her cleavage being so very exposed. Tastefully pinned to one side was a tiny little snowflake pin.

"Well at least it's snowing somewhere, huh?" David said bitterly from the couch. He hadn't forgiven her. The look he gave her frightened her. If he said something about the knife, she didn't know what she'd do.

"You look gorgeous, honey," her dad said, rising to plant a soft kiss on her cheek. There were some flowers in her hair, but it was down, not an up-do.

"Fit for a millionaire's party, I think," her mother said. Her mom looked so very proud of herself. She had applied the make-up, she had done her daughter's hair. Alice had grudgingly let her do everything, even though it made her feel more and more exposed every second. There was, thankfully, a knock on the door before her mother could fawn over her anymore.

Her dad opened the door and greeted Adam while her mother touched up an out-of-place hair. Her smile was enough to make Alice want to disappear. It was the first time Alice had even had the mild courage to wear make-up, and the red in her cheeks said everything as Adam looked her up and down. He smiled approvingly. He hadn't seen this dress.

"I'm sorry we don't have time to chat. We're running a little late." Adam said guardedly.

"Oh well, then, hurry out, honey." Her mother handed her the little handbag Alice was borrowing and threw a black wrap over her bare shoulders. Little did her mother know that inside the purse was a knife as well as her I.D. and invitation. Not that she even needed that. Everyone in town knew who she was by now, especially since her impromptu make-over. It was still strange to her that she needed a knife to go to a fancy millionaire's party. She got into the car with Adam as quickly as she could on heels.

"We're not late," she said as he started the car. It would be a three-minute drive.

"No, it's a trick. Parents never pay attention to time when their child is dressed to the nines. I just didn't want to stand there feeling like a high-schooler while your mother fawned over you." Alice laughed, then suddenly got serious again.

"I have to talk to Brassila." The car screeched to a halt.

"What?" he asked, trying to recover from the shock.

"You know, a week ago when I met you on the boat asking about my family...well, David found the knife. He wants to know what's going on. I told him that I'd tell him on his birthday, which is only a week away. I had to say something." For a moment, Adam looked like he was really fond of the idea of beating his head against the steering wheel.

"You couldn't have told me about this when I took you shopping? In fact, I want to know how you can stay away from people as much as you do and still cause as many problems as you do."

"I'm gifted at attracting trouble," she said, that dead sound creeping back into her voice. Adam didn't answer; he wasn't about to touch that one, he still didn't know exactly what had happened to her. He knew she had to have been raped; the way she reacted to certain things was typical of rape victims. Then there were other things, like the knife, and her grandmother. She always tried to keep the knife as far from her as possible. He wasn't stupid; he could put a few things together without her telling him the details.

"David…"

"Didn't tell our parents, but he's not stupid either. He knows there's something weird about the knife, that it's not normal."

Adam sighed, pulling his car slowly onto the beach. He was tense. He watched shadows crawling from the surf like monsters in a cheesy creature feature. The guests were arriving. He was attending a fish party and he was likely the only human; this couldn't possibly go wrong. He turned off the ignition and put earplugs in his ears.

"What are those for?" Alice asked.

"Remember the whole thing about singing I told you?"

"Yeah?"

"This deadens the sound enough so that it won't affect me and I can still keep some semblance of a rational mind. Noise-cancelling. It works, I swear."

She looked up at him terrified, "There's going to be singing?"

"Everyone sings at a fish party—except, of course, me," he smiled. Alice didn't return his smile. She knew it was coming before the words came out of his mouth: she would have to sing. He ignored her fear as he stepped out and walked around the car to open Alice's door. For a second, Alice didn't move, she just stared ahead at the ghostly figures. She took a deep breath, then took his proffered hand.

Adam led her into the party, where they were properly announced as they came in from the beach entrance. "Local Doctor, Adam Carson, and the transform, Alice Bailey." Every head within hearing distance turned to stare directly at her. There was the "transform" word again. She hardly recognized a single face. Plus, bringing a human to the party certainly wasn't common. No one hid their stares, nor did they hide their guarded whispers. Alice felt like running for the beach screaming at the top of her lungs.

"Don't worry, it's going to get worse," Adam said, applying pressure to her hand. She stared at him angrily as he escorted her to the floor where people were dancing. It was a wide open, classic ballroom, with one wall lined with floor-to-ceiling mirrors that looked out over the ocean. It was beautiful.

"That's supposed to make me feel better?" Alice whispered fiercely, ignoring the splendor that embraced her. She felt claustrophobic in the mass of people that surrounded her, stared at her as she danced with the doctor. There was a live band on stage and someone was singing with them, "Black Magic Woman." There was a karaoke-style setup, but apparently no one was bad. Some were better than others, but everyone could sing.

"It's a folk thing. Singing is always important, and, on land, dancing is equally important." He said, sending her into a twirl, admiring the way the dress fell around her. The song was changing and someone else was moving up to the stage. Alice saw a flash of blond hair.

"Finn?"

"Everyone sings. You'll be expected to sing, too." Alice looked up, cursing him in her mind. That was not something she really wanted to be reminded of. The footwork wasn't bad for Alice but Adam was having trouble as Finn broke into song. Alice looked up.

"Imagine me and you, I do, / I think about you day and night, it's only right." So many people were smiling at Finn. His voice filled the room with a charm that made the temperature rise. It was so unlike his personality. Behind the charm, Alice recognized an air of distaste in his voice. It was a romantic song, but he was putting no feeling into it whatsoever; to him, it was just a chore, though he made it sound convincing enough. As Adam spun her again, Alice found herself following Finn. He wasn't looking at her; he wasn't looking at anyone. That hidden sadness, Alice knew, was the emotion of losing yourself, put straight into song. It put her off guard to understand him so well. She knew that was how the language of the folk worked, but no one expressed that emotion but her. She looked around and could tell no one else heard it. They were just enjoying the song. Alice caught a flash of blond highlights in the crowd and noticed Ashley was near the stage, her eyes glowing, like she was certain he was singing just for her. There were glassy eyes everywhere, enjoying the song, not noticing the mournful undercurrents beneath.

"Finn's expected to dance with everyone tonight, including visitors. My guess is, he probably won't be easy to find after his song." As Adam spoke Alice almost jumped, then turned back to her date. "Alice, you should probably sing next."

"Um, Adam? I only sing in the shower. I would rather go dead last, after most everyone has left."

"Are you bad?"

"Well, I don't know, I guess. I've never sung in front of anyone! David always complained, but he's my little brother; he's required to."

"Come on, you'll go next." Alice bristled as he moved her into position.

"What do I sing?" she whispered fiercely. It was too late. Finn was turning to leave, going down the stairs on the opposite side of the stage. Others were ushering her up, and the band looked at her expectantly. They must know thousands of songs to have been able to do this with karaoke. She looked out at the audience; they was expecting her to open her mouth any moment. Ashley was suppressing giggles. She had found her friends among the crowd and they were, of course, laughing with her. It seemed like there were more of them than usual, one of them sporting a fresh scar across one of her eyes.

This was not what Alice had been expecting. As if the dress

wasn't bad enough, now she had to perform, too. The look that Ashley gave her made Alice's blood run cold and wiped every song she possibly could have thought of from her mind, so Alice turned to the band and said the first song that came to her mind. The song that had introduced her to this extremely messed up town. "Mr. Sandman."

A couple of people walked up to other mikes as her back-up singers. She caught sight of white-blond hair and suddenly Tommy was up on the stage between two women. This was not, this was not, *oh fuck.*

"Mr. Sandman, bring me a dream, / Make him the cutest that I've ever seen." Ashley's face fell immediately. Several of the older people in the room were smiling at her. It was a pleasant change from the looks she had been getting after walking in with a human. She looked over at Tommy and saw his familiar smirk. He was dancing with the bassist, until he put in that "Yes?" She cringed but didn't stop, she just looked away from Tommy's piercing gaze. It seemed like he knew more than anyone else in the room.

She caught a glimpse of Finn trying to escape as carefully as he could. He didn't want people to notice that he was slipping away, and she was helping him. No one was looking at him. Everyone was transfixed on the transform, the newest transform that any of them had heard. It wasn't going badly; she could see Adam smiling up at her. So she began to get into it a little. It was almost fun.

"And lots of wavy hair like Liberace!" She threw her head to the side, her hair bobbing along. It was adorable, endearing even. She was singing herself into the hearts of these people she didn't want any part of. A chill ran up Adam's spine as he watched her finish the song. Though she sang with all her heart, there was something he didn't like in it, something that that made his skin crawl.

As the band segued into a filler song, Alice stared out over the smiling crowd. She awkwardly gave up the mic and got off the stage as quick as she could, managing to avoid the people trying to praise her as she stepped down. She slipped through the audience and disappeared as fast as she could. It wasn't just the embarrassment of having sung in front of an audience: she had to catch Finn. He had very adeptly used the distraction she had created, and she had to catch up with him. He was the only one who could take her to Brassila. He was outside already, peeling off his tux jacket, unbuttoning his pants, heading for the ocean.

"Finn! Wait."

He spun, furious. "What do you want?"

She almost turned away. He was so angry, so desperate to escape.

"How's your grandmother?" she asked sheepishly. He looked at her suspiciously, looking for some hint of sarcasm.

"She's alive still, hanging on."

"That makes her the clan leader right? I need to talk to her," she paused as his eyes narrowed. "David, my little brother, found my knife. He wants to know what's going on." Finn's eyes flared. To most people, he would have said they were stupidly careless and deserved anything that they got for making such a big mistake. But he knew, like no one else, how Alice felt about knives.

"Fine, follow me," he said, buttoning his pants back up. He was still wearing his shirt, which made Alice smile. Shirts just weren't Finn's style, at least not when buttoned. He left his jacket on the sand. Alice figured he probably didn't care; he likely owned the tux and could afford another.

They slipped into the back entrance, near the enormous kitchen. Alice had to stop herself from gawking. They could hear the party, but it was far away. Finn was guiding her in a way that avoided being discovered by anyone else. They headed up a set of stairs that squeaked. Finn flinched at every noise, though there was no way anyone in the ballroom could hear them.

Alice had never been in a house this large. Without him as a guide, she knew she'd get lost, and was further affirmed in this belief when, on the third story, he opened a wall. She couldn't have guessed there were seams there if she hadn't seen him open it. If there were more hidden rooms, she'd never be able to find her way around.

The room inside was dim, and there was a woman lying on

a bed at the focal point. She looked frail, like she would fall apart at any moment. Her eyes were a deep brown, like Tommy's, and her hair was long and stark white. She was old, but Alice could see her undimmed beauty. Even time could not take this woman down. This was the woman Matthew had loved, the woman on whom he had spent endless amounts of money building a town in the middle of nowhere. Time seemed to slow down.

"Finn," Brassila breathed. Alice felt immediately uncomfortable and knew that she didn't belong. She wanted to run in the other direction, but she couldn't. David's life was on the line. For a moment she understood how Finn could be upset about the woman in the bed dying in front of his eyes. This wasn't the quick death her grandmother had. This woman was dying slowly, alone, away from her clan, but still forced to be a part of it. She was a matriarch.

"Grandma, I've brought the new transform. She would like to ask permission to tell an outsider. Her brother," he said, giving Alice a poisonous look. When he turned back to Brassila and moved to the side of the bed, his face softened. It was an expression Alice had never seen on Finn.

"Come here, Miss Bailey." Alice moved closer. She could do nothing else; the woman commanded respect. Brassila took her hand as Alice sunk into a plush chair beside the bed. "The question is not a yes-or-no question. Your brother as much one of us as you are; he just doesn't know it yet. I hear you have a voice as prized as your grandmother."

"My grandmother?" Alice looked around the room. There was a flat screen TV showing Brassila the entire party, playing softly. Kari was on stage now, singing some Britney Spears song and looking for someone, probably Finn.

"Emma, your grandmother. She fell for a soldier and was exiled when she chose to marry him and begin living a human life. She was no clan leader; she was just a maid with a beautiful voice." Brassila sighed, her chest rising and falling almost straight into the bed. "I knew her once."

Finn looked surprised. "Grandma?"

"You look so much like her," she said, ignoring her grandson. "In my younger days, I met her. She was a Wanderlust, a mer without a clan. I wanted to be like her. For a while, we swam together, until she found Mickey," she looked at Alice with those deep, penetrating eyes, "You are new but your bloodline is old. In this house there are histories of folk from all over the world. Volumes upon volumes, dating back further than I can tell. My clan used to number around five hundred, but in my lifetime we are now one-fifth that size. Humans scar the sea and the folk can do nothing about it. They must not know of us, and there are so few of us now. We lose so many to the temptations that land has to offer: technology, and men," she said sadly. "You," she paused, dragging in a labored breath, "You are as true as any of the other maids your age. You loved water from an early age, yes?" Alice didn't have to answer. She thought back to her swim meets, her grandmother always cheering her on but never going near the water herself. Now Alice knew exactly why.

When her grandma went to the ocean, she had always kept a respectful distance while Alice played in and out of the waves. It was because she had to, because she couldn't go into the water! She couldn't risk her kind. It was so startling to Alice, this new information, that she could hardly keep her brain processing everything that Brassila was saying. From a population of five hundred down to one hundred, in a span of only eighty or a hundred years. Alice marveled, looking at the frail old woman.

"There are so few males compared to the women. In some tribes, the ratio is five to one. It makes sense that a maid would look to the land for a husband, but it is almost a crime to take the water from those who love it as much as your grandmother. Young Bailey. Downstairs is my clan, and many visiting from others. Some just visiting, some looking for mates," she paused and turned to Finn. "How many women are down there chasing you, Finn?" she asked slyly. Brassila knew her grandsons. She knew how much Finn avoided the other girls, avoided everyone in general, but she wouldn't punish him. She knew, in time, Finn would learn, as she had learned, that you can't get through your troubles alone. On land, humans surrounded themselves with people, with friends, with family. Mer were also social creatures, but the sea was such a lonely place. Maybe Finn wouldn't learn before she left, but she had faith in him.

"Ten of them," Finn answered bitterly. Brassila tried to laugh, but it was so weak. Alice could smell the death in the room, but the woman wore it so well. For a moment, Alice almost felt sorry for Finn. Maybe it was easier to watch someone go quickly than to see a loved one suffer.

"I do not think I will see you mate, Finn," Brassila smiled weakly at him, as if it were an effort even to force the muscles of her face to make an expression. "Did you bring your knife, young Alice?" Alice pulled it out of her purse and showed it to the woman. "Finn, go to the drawer in that dresser and bring me the box inside."

Finn obliged his grandmother dutifully. "You do not need that curved blade," she said as she opened the box carefully. In it lay a sheathed knife barely visible in a hairnet studded with pearls. Brassila picked it up and handed it to the younger woman. Alice stared: it was just like the one in her dream. "Take it, my dear. Your grandmother was a truer friend to me than anyone. It is a woman's blade, and, alas, my only heirs are men." Alice continued to look at the knife, then realized that it was with much effort that the old woman was still holding it aloft. Finn stared at them both, wide-eyed. "Go on, my dear," prompted Brassila. Gently, Alice took the blade from her wrinkled hands. The net was intricately knotted and studded with jewels, and the hilt held an emerald the size of Alice's thumb. Alice was startled speechless. She looked at

Finn, who did not return her gaze. It obviously irked him that his grandmother was passing this to her. Alice had a feeling that the passing of a blade meant more to the folk than she could understand.

"I...I can't take this." Alice replied meekly as the blade sat in her hands.

Brassila found Alice's eyes, "You can and you will." The statement left no room for further arguments. This woman was strong, even in her deathbed. "I know you will keep it well," Brassila continued. "You are a strong woman, Alice Bailey. I am proud to have you as part of my clan. Bring your brother to this beach and show him. Let him make his own decision, just as you will eventually make yours." She turned her face away from Alice and looked up at Finn again. Alice suddenly had the feeling that she was completely out of place. Brassila smiled as she squeezed her grandson's hand. A current passed through her body. Alice watched as her eyes fluttered closed. She said nothing, Finn said nothing. She could no longer see Brassila's chest moving up and down. They knew she was gone. Alice had just witnessed the passing of a titan.

She stood, horrified. She felt so much for this woman she had only just met. It was all so very confusing, and if she weren't frozen on the spot, she would have backed away reflexively. She could do nothing but stand there in silence, fighting the emotions that threatened her.

"Leave." Finn said, so low that Alice barely heard it. Alice tripped over her heels as she turned, leaving Finn alone with his dead grandmother.

Somehow, she found her way, stumbling, back to the ballroom. She leaned against the wall, then stuffed the hairnet that was still in her hand into her purse. There were tears on her cheek and sobs in her chest. She would give anything to be as strong as that woman had been. She felt like she was going to slip to the floor, like her legs just weren't there anymore and there was no fin to replace them.

"Alice!" Adam noticed her suddenly, then hastily put his arm around her. He was nearly lifting her, taking her out of sight of prying eyes. She was on a bench outside now and he was holding a Kleenex in front of her. He didn't say anything; he knew what had happened. He knew how weak Brassila was. "Calm down, it's okay," he said, idly stroking her hair. He pulled her close to him, holding her shaking form in his arms.

Finn came down the stairs, and looked at her disdainfully. Adam looked up at him angrily, though Alice didn't even notice, her face buried in Adam's chest. Finn ignored them both and went to find Tommy.

"I have to dance, don't I?" Alice whispered as she calmed. He looked down at her, brushing an errant hair from her eyes.

"It would be better. You should be seen." She let him lift her up and lead her to the dance floor but she didn't feel the music;

she simply went through the motions. She was used to it by now, always going through the motions, feeling weak and vulnerable all the time. She didn't want to be seen; she wanted to fade away, she wanted to retreat. All the make-up, the hairstyling, it felt like she was carrying fifty extra pounds. Shut out the sounds, shut out the smells, shut out the light, breathe. But it didn't work, she knew it wouldn't, she was in too deep.

Before she knew it, before she could register anything, Tommy cut in with a simple tap on Adam's shoulder. She could tell he knew about Brassila, but his smirk was still there. Alice was very nearly offended by the sudden change of dance partners. She sent a warning spark into Tommy's hands as they continued to dance. She looked around for the first time, catching sight of Finn. He looked like he was in pain, dancing with some girl or another.

"You have spirit. I just thought I should warn you," Tommy said, pulling her out of her thoughts.

"Warn me of what?"

"Be careful of the good doctor."

"What?"

"He is falling head over heels for you as we speak." Alice stared at Tommy. She could hardly believe him. "Just saying, human and mer. You could lose the ocean." She stole a glance at the doctor. She felt tenderness for him that she hadn't realized was there, but it wasn't anything Alice wanted. Tenderness meant she had a connection to him, and connections made her weak. Besides, none of it was Tommy's business anyway. She tried to pull away from Tommy but his grip was too strong.

"We will send Brassila to the sea after the party. I thought you might want to be there." Finally he broke away, giving her a sarcastic bow, and Adam swept into his place. Alice felt a strange relief. He looked irritated, but he wasn't about to say anything. He shouldn't even be there; it was a party for fish, not for him. He had no real desire to be a part of this world.

Alice was distracted. She could hear Brassila's soft voice echoing through her memory. *You are strong, Alice Bailey.* Alice didn't feel strong. Alice felt like screaming again. Alice felt like disappearing forever, running away. Yet here was Adam. He was anchoring her, not to mention her parents. How could she think of disappearing when they were thinking they finally had their daughter back. And what of David? She thought of David, of his future, of their past together. Suddenly she missed him so much.

Memories of them played across her mind's eye as Adam led her around and around. Her actions were mechanical; it was her mind that was truly dancing. For the first time, she felt acutely the loss of her kid brother, the boy who used to be her best friend. Soon, it would change, one way or another.

She looked up as she realized that Adam was stepping away, nodding his head to Finn. Finn, who looked so unhappy. She saw for the first time how much he wanted to escape, just as much as she did. He took her hands, but he was stiff. He was shut off to her and she was shut off to him. They swirled around the floor under the stares of the other mer. Everyone was watching Finn, and now he was with the transform. Alice even caught a glimpse of Ashley's glare, though it didn't register. She heard the slamming of a door, but it didn't matter, Finn wasn't there any more than she was.

Alice broke the silence. "Why sad?" she asked, below anyone's hearing but her partner's. He stared at her, not understanding. "In your song, there was sadness, something no one else seemed to hear." She didn't truly care, but the curiosity was eating at her. She knew that emotion all too well, the one he sang.

He stared at her, and stood for a couple extra seconds after the song had ended. He stared at her, but he didn't answer. Abruptly, he turned tail and fled. He pushed through the throng of people, away from the other groping maids, and disappeared out the door.

Chapter 14

Brassila

Alice stood behind a carefully placed potted plant in a corner. She had run from Adam, had run from the stares of the other folk. Parties weren't really her scene anymore, no matter how much champagne she imbibed. She just she couldn't breathe. Out of her purse she pulled the hairnet and stared into the pearls. She saw Brassila's eyes and her insistence, felt the mer's courage and current. Her hands were shaking when she remembered the reflection of a pair of green eyes not unlike her own. She looked up, suddenly seeing the face of a little girl watching her.

"You," Alice said. The little girl kept looking at Alice, but made no response. "You were the one that led me back here on the day I became one of you." The little girl cocked her head to one side and nodded.

"My name is Aria," she said, almost so softly Alice could hardly hear. "You were there. With the grandmother." Alice stared at her wide eyes. Her dark hair wasn't bound in any way; in fact, she was by far the least primped and pampered person there, and certainly the youngest. She lifted her slight hands to point at the hairnet in Alice's hands. Alice knelt to be on a level with the young mer. She was so small that the dress she was wearing didn't remotely fit her; a little waif, swimming in a cloud of material. She definitely looked like she would be more at home beneath the waves. Something about her made Alice respond to her.

"Where are your parents?"

Gently, Aria took the hairnet, then moved behind Alice and began to undo Alice's hair. Alice couldn't figure the child out; she was shy, and, yet, she was forward. She began to carefully style Alice's hair into the net, with the hilt of the knife pinning it back. The blade was hidden in the hair and it was impossible to guess that the decorated hilt belonged to a blade.

"Mom and Dad wander. When Tommy returned, my parents left, to continue his mission." She moved around to Alice's front, watching her curiously. She brushed a lock of wet, mousy brown hair from her eyes.

"Why did they leave you?" Aria watched her.

"I don't…understand?" she said.

"Your parents. How could they leave their daughter?"

"I have many parents here," Aria said simply. Alice stared at the little girl, wondering what her life was like. She was born of the ocean and the clan and grew with the ocean. Alice had been born of land, and the ocean had claimed her. Instead of dealing with the concept, she stood and moved across the hall to a giant decorative mirror. She gasped as she stared at her reflection, Aria standing behind her. Alice hardly recognized the woman in the

163

mirror. She was no longer the happy-go-lucky person she had been in college, nor was she the visage of death she had been for the past two years. She was beautiful, but there was a hint of danger to her, too, and her blond hair was perfectly complimented by the embroidered hairnet, with only one errant lock hanging over her forehead. She looked down at the little girl.

"Thank you."

Aria looked up at her. Her small hand reached up to point at Alice's heart. "We are different. I am young, and you are new." Alice looked at the girl staring back at her and knew exactly what she meant. They were both different from the others, similar in their differences. Alice realized that Aria was the only young mer there, possibly the youngest in the world. Just as Alice was an example of something that hadn't happened in centuries, so might this girl be similarly rare. Alice reflexively let the current run across her fingers as she brushed the long brown hair behind the little girl's ear, trying to contemplate what exactly that meant. She wondered if that was what the other folk wondered about, too.

"Alice! There you are." Alice looked up to see Adam at the end of the hallway. She heard Aria patter off behind her. Adam's eyes grew wide as he looked at the woman in front of him.

The pearls, the knife nestled in her hair, it was all wrong. He clenched his hands. She didn't look human; she wasn't human, but she was beautiful. It pulled at the strings of his heart. Maybe he had just been around the folk too long. Despite the earplugs, the language of the folk had to be getting to him. He shook off the unwanted emotions and strode forward, taking her hand. She did not resist.

"They're sending Brassila off," he said simply. She looked up at him. Her eyes matched the emerald on the hilt of the knife. She nodded and Adam led her through the crowd and out to the beach. There were stares, there were whispers, but Alice didn't notice any of it.

Adam stood next to her, holding her hand. She didn't push him away. Tommy was standing there, too, a solemn look on his face, his spiked hair blowing like grass in the ocean breeze. There were a couple others that Alice didn't recognize. Misa was there. She looked suspiciously at Alice and Adam holding hands. It was not a large gathering; most of the mer remained inside the building, ignoring the small group on the beach.

Alice watched Finn carry his grandmother from the house and down to the ocean. He gently set her down in the surf. To Alice's astonishment, as the water touched her, she melted into it as foam. Adam was looking down; he couldn't see well enough anyway. Finn walked back to the house, not even acknowledging the group on the sand that had shown up to pay their respects. Like a stubborn child, he slammed the door behind him. The crowd slowly dispersed.

"We should go," Adam said quietly

"You go," she said, "I'll walk." He nodded in resignation

and Alice stood there while everyone disappeared around her. There was nothing of Brassila left, except in her progeny: a sarcastic, sardonic little boy, and an asshole of an older grandson; that was all Brassila left behind. That, and the knife nestled so perfectly in Alice's hair. She stared at the ocean and thought of David, and how he had found the other knife.

A hand fell to her shoulder and she jumped. She spun on the boy standing behind her on the empty beach.

"Tommy!" she said.

"Who else? Expecting the doctor? I believe he was tired of dancing with us fishies." She scowled. Tommy was not someone she could trust. He looked out at the ocean. "It wasn't wise for her to bequeath you with her knife."

"What do you mean?"

"Oh, nothing," he smiled that evil smile at her.

"What do you want?"

"We have business, and I know my delightful sibling will not handle it."

"What…?"

"Brassila's last decree. You have an obligation to share our secret. Your brother, I believe." She stared at him, then looked to the house. To her surprise, it was almost empty. She had no idea how long she had been standing there. "You've been here quite a while, you know," he said, following her gaze. "Dawn is almost here, and, ceremony-wise, that's really when this should happen. Not that I'm much for ceremony." He crossed his arms over his chest and smirked at her. Part of her wanted to slap the smirk off his face, but her only response was a nod. She turned slowly on Tommy, though she didn't like the idea of him being behind her, and started the trek home.

She walked home in a daze. She knew precisely what she was going to do, exactly what Tommy had meant. She knew exactly where she was going, and she knew what it would mean. This could be the end or the beginning for her brother. She tried to find comfort in Adam's words: *Your brother probably is.* Somehow that didn't make her feel much better. Still, she snuck upstairs. The steps didn't even creak; she was learning to use her weight differently, she was becoming more and more like them. She slipped into David's bedroom and shook him.

He looked up groggily. "Alice, what are you doing?"

She put her finger to her lips, shushing him and handing him a shirt. He put it on slowly. "It's five o'clock in the morning!"

"Don't wake Mom and Dad, just come with me." He flopped back on his bed and closed his eyes.

"It's too early," he mumbled into his pillow.

"You're up this late all the time! Come on," she reached forward and gave him a little shock. His eyes opened wide and he stared straight at her. For the first time, he noticed what she looked like through the make-up. He looked at her hair, covered by a hairnet encrusted with pearls, finished off by a hair stick with a giant emerald in it. She didn't look like his sister: there was something different in her eyes, her skin was different; something wasn't right about her.

"You shocked me! How did you do that?"

"Come on, I'll show you," she whispered back.

David got up, staring at her, wondering. She threw his swim trunks at him. He looked at her suspiciously as she turned away and he put them on. She was hurrying quietly out the door of his bedroom. She wasn't even making a sound, and he knew that those floors creaked. He grabbed a flashlight and slipped into some sandals.

The two siblings snuck out of the house together. Alice was in front leading the way, with David trailing behind, watching her in a way he hadn't since her hair was cut. He cringed every time his feet creaked on the stairs. She moved so much more swiftly, looking back at him, irritated at his slow pace. He was making a great effort to make no sound, but she was moving like a ghost. Something about this was so strange, even in this strange town, and yet Alice seemed so strong, like she knew exactly what she was doing. Exiting the broke into a run and he followed; they were running down to the beach together. It was the first time in a while they had done something together, yet somehow it felt wrong. Alice ran, tears welling in her eyes. How could David possibly know that she might be leading him to his death? They were now running past the signs warning that trespassers would be shot.

"Aly, we're not supposed to be here," David said, slowing down. Alice was ahead of him, pulling the nice slinky dress above her head. It landed near a discarded tux jacket. Under her dress, she was wearing a bathing suit. This was one he hadn't seen before, it was deep blue. David looked up at the giant wall of windows that looked into to the ballroom. There was a boy his age standing there, drinking a cup of some drink or another. His brown eyes watched the two of them. "Alice!" he said with alarm. "There's someone watching."

Alice looked back, the moonlight shined off her green eyes in a way that David couldn't believe was normal. He looked back with her; the moonlight glinted off the boy's eyes, too. "It's Tommy," she said.

"One of the Caraways?"

"The younger," she nodded.

He joined her, switching on the flashlight and shining it around. There didn't seem to be anything remarkable about this beach; it looked just like the public one, only more secluded. "Alice, what are we doing on a millionaire's private beach at 5 am, dressed in swimwear?" He felt nervous, especially with Tommy watching their every move, but no one was shooting. Alice must have permission to be here – after all, the Christmas party must have just finished.

She smiled at him. "I'm a mermaid, Davy." He spun to look at her. He stared at her like she was insane as she ran into the surf. She didn't give him time to process her comment, and he certainly didn't believe it. David wasn't about to move to join her. This all had to be some trick. Alice was under the waves where he couldn't see her. He shined his flashlight on the water nervously as he waited far too long for her to surface, growing more scared by the second. He caught sight of the bottoms of her bathing suit, washing up in the surf, ripped. He moved forward and gently picked them up. He still didn't understand what was going on.

Suddenly Alice shot out of the water at high speed—with a tail! David jumped back, dropping the swimsuit into the water. She hit the water again and then let herself wash up on the beach, her tail extended behind her.

David fell down on his ass.

There was no other reaction he had for it. The flashlight fell on the sand at his feet. "How is this? What is this? What?" Tommy suddenly went flashing past him. David blinked. Tommy wasn't wearing anything except a belt with a short sword in it. A sword? Tommy was running naked for the waves with a sword strapped to his hip. Tommy leapt into the waves, then came back with a tail, same as Alice.

David's mouth hung open like in the old Looney Toons. He just couldn't believe what his eyes were seeing, but the flashlight was shimmering off their scales. He couldn't even form words anymore.

"Grandma was a mermaid, David. That's why she never went in the water with us as kids."

"That...doesn't...make sense," he mumbled "Grandma?"

"She couldn't go into the water. She was forbidden. Both for the tail, and because she fell for a human." That wasn't exactly what David had meant. None of it made sense. Mermaids weren't real, but there Tommy was, staring at him with that sarcastic gaze. Staring at him, laughing at David's expression with his eyes. It was all widely disconcerting, far too much for his sleep-addled brain to understand.

David looked back at Alice, perplexed. "You—how long?" he demanded, suddenly angry.

"About a month after we moved here, when I decided to take a swim."

"You...you didn't..." his hands shook. How could she keep something like this from him? This was it, this was the secret, this was the reason she had started changing, and here he was, sitting in the dark. What did she want from him? What did she expect from him? He shook his head and opened his eyes again. This time he stared at Tommy.

"A touch of any merfolk's tail will open up the gills in your nose and mouth and change you, as long as you carry the gene," Tommy put in, unhelpfully. He also gave David a look that he didn't like at all. It was a look that made David feel like he should run away from this revelation right now.

"His brother was swimming past," Alice continued.

"He hated you then, by the way," Tommy said, turning toward her, interrupting again. Alice felt awkward, having just seen the little brother in his birthday suit. Maybe it was something left over from when she was human; logically, it made more sense than wasting a pair of trunks every time. Alice hardly heard what he said.

"That's how you met the Caraways? The Caraways are fish? I'm a fish?" David didn't seem to be processing the information, Alice was reminded of her own trouble with it. "I just... I... Alice, I role play! Stuff like this isn't real."

"It's real, David." He looked at her, looking for help. She was calm, perfectly calm, and Tommy was eyeing him like he could be on a dinner plate. If Alice had been excited, if she had been sad, he would have run away screaming. He was reminded of times when they were kids at Grandma's house and Grandma would watch as David and his sister went in and out of the waves, him on stubby legs chasing his adept bigger sister, or riding on her back as she swam like a dolphin. He missed those times. He had been so caught up in his computer games ever since Alice had gotten back from Grandma's after Grandma died. When Alice came back, it was as if she was an oyster that had been scooped of pearl and meat alike, and the shell smashed with a hammer. He buried himself deeper in the games when he realized his sister wasn't really there anymore, and she didn't seem to be ever coming back. He looked at her now with her bright green eyes shining brightly like they used to, before their family had been spontaneously torn apart.

David trusted Alice. He didn't understand anything she was telling him, and he certainly didn't trust the young Caraway, but he trusted her. He didn't know how any of it was possible, but he trusted her. David slowly inched toward the water. Tommy moved away into the depths and David jumped a little. The presence of the younger Caraway with his short sword made him nervous.

"David, if you touch it, you'll have a tail any time you submerge yourself in water." She didn't add that if he couldn't grow a tail, Tommy would likely murder him right then and there. "You could never go to a pool party or play with your friends in the ocean. You can't tell Mom and Dad. It would just be us." David looked up at her seriously.

"Aly, you've been my big sister since I was born. We never had anything between us until you went away to Grandma's. You were sad before you left, but when you came back you weren't even there anymore. Then we move to this armpit and after a couple months, I can see you again, but it's like I'm on the outside looking in. I can see you, but I can't reach you. I'd give anything just to be your little brother again."

He was close now. She reached up and ruffled his hair as he

leaned down. "You're not as stupid as you look, little brother. I love you, you know." He looked up at her, startled. He knew there was something she wasn't telling him; there was fear in her eyes. He kneeled in the surf next to her, staring at the tail that had never been a part of his sister before.

His hand climbed away from his body against his will. He reached for where her legs should be as she watched him intently. His hand came into contact with the slimy surface of her tail. He pulled back immediately, but it was enough. He felt the current running through him, and then it burned. It burned bad. Tommy smiled his sardonic smile and moved beneath the water; he grabbed Alice's tail. Alice realizing what he was doing, grabbed David's feet, and together they dragged David in the water so fast he had no choice but to breathe in the water. He didn't drown. He was breathing water, breathing through gills, gills that had opened and burned in the coastal air.

He looked at Alice through eyes that could see through the murky seawater. Tommy was behind her. He had a smirk on his face, as if daring David to catch him. There was a small forest of kelp behind them in the shallow water. It looked like fun as Tommy zipped into it. Alice smiled at David, her relief palpable as she followed Tommy. David looked down at himself: tail, fins, webbing between his fingers. He smiled and was after Alice like a shot.

It was unlike anything he had experienced ever before; the

life around him, the invigorating feeling of being a fish *in* water. His sister alive and well and with him, playing with him. Even Tommy was fun. They weren't talking to each other, but he didn't feel like he couldn't. Tommy started singing, but it wasn't like a song on land. It was like some mellow instrument. Tommy was singing a song of challenge. David knew, knew instinctively, this must be how they communicated to each other in the water. He was a mer, part of a species with a history unknown to those people walking on land. He wondered how he had ever endured being tied to a flat plane, because moving in three dimensions was just so easy.

Down, down, down as fast as they could go, all three of them traveling so fast that they were bullets speeding past the life around them. Up, up, up, up, up: it was insane, the speed, the feel of the water streaming across his scales, Alice's hair with the pearls gleaming in it, then they were out! Air! Down again! A little girl joined them, smiling her greeting to David. Others slowly began to join the game. It was nighttime and the folk were so far out to sea that no humans could see them. Dawn was only barely breaking over the ocean. It was the one time that the folk were free to move as they wished, to move like what they were, lords of the ocean. There were dolphins joining them; they were so playful, joining the dance. It was more than David ever could have imagined. Then Alice sang. It was happy and sad all at the same time. David joined her, with a song of pure delight. Happy that they were all together again, he sang a song of rebirth, renewal, and reunion. All of a

175

sudden, David had a place where he could enjoy himself, where he belonged.

Alice leapt from the water and he leapt with her. They met in the air and grabbed at each other; they were hugging in midair, and then, with a splash, they were beneath the surface again. There was another girl there, a cute one who couldn't be much older than David. Her hair was red and she had a huge smile on her face. He danced with her, he danced with Tommy, he danced with Alice, all in an environment that no human could ever see. Despite his ties to the land, right then, at that moment, this felt more right than anything in the world.

Alice thought of Brassila, the titan, the matriarch, the amazing woman who had worn her knife in the plaits of her hair and stolen the heart of a young millionaire. She thought of her grandmother. She wondered how it was possible to give up this feeling. She knew this was right: her brother, the ocean, the night, and the memory of a great woman she could only strive to emulate.

David would dream of that moment for years and years. It was the first moment he knew he had his sister back. He was surrounded by people who didn't think he was inept at everything. He was accepted and at home in those coastal waters, and he was free.

Tommy watched the two of them together. It was almost heartwarming. He was glad he didn't have to spill blood this night. He touched the hilt of the short sword, fingering the thumb-sized emerald and watching its mate twinkling amid Alice's hair. All the young mer were there, dancing in the rising sun, except two. Tommy knew exactly what it meant, but he didn't see any reason to interrupt the two transforms. They would discover their destinies in their own time. For now, he smirked.

Chapter 15

Dinner and a Show

Alice walked down the road on a mission. It had been a couple of days since she had abandoned Adam, and she owed him an explanation. She reached her hand up to knock on his door and stopped when the door opened. She smelled dinner cooking in the house. She looked at Adam quizzically.

"No, I had no idea you were coming," he said sarcastically. "Come on in, I'm making dinner."

She didn't move. "I owe you an apology."

"Apology accepted. Come on in!" he said eagerly. She looked him up and down. The food did smell good. She figured it wouldn't hurt to share dinner with him; she did owe him for what he had put up with at the party. He sat down on a plush green couch and she sat in a nearby armchair, which nearly swallowed her. She wondered why he didn't get a new set of furniture.

"I was rude. I'm sorry." Alice continued.

"You had to deal with fish stuff, Aly. I understand." He reached forward to grab her hand, but she pulled it away.

"No one calls me Aly but my family." She didn't know

why it grated her so much but it did.

"Ummm," he mumbled folding his hands in his lap, "So, David?"

"Obviously alive,"

"He's,"

"Like me, yeah." Adam frowned, but quickly tried to hide it from her. Before he could decide what to say next, they were abruptly interrupted by the oven timer. Adam hastily got up to fetch it out.

"What are you cooking, anyway?" Alice asked.

"Pepper-crusted lamb with plum chutney."

"This, coming from the guy who didn't expect company?"

He peeked out from the kitchen, "Nope, didn't expect it at all." He smiled one of his disarming smiles at her and all was forgiven. She enjoyed his company, however awkward the situation might be lately. He had a habit of disarming any situation.

Suddenly, a loud knock came at the door.

Adam looked up. "I wasn't expecting any more company…you didn't bring David, did you?"

"No," she said. "I'll get it if you're busy."

"Yeah, if you could, I'd appreciate it."

Alice pulled herself out of the armchair and padded noiselessly across the carpet to the door. She reached her hand forward to the handle, opened it, and suddenly jumped back.

The knife cut through the air where her face had been only moments ago. There was no time to think, only time to act, though she was nothing but surprised.

She fell backwards into the table, sending a lamp crashing to the floor.

"Alice!" Adam ran out of the kitchen, then stopped in his tracks.

Alice blocked the next thrust, her arm against her attacker's. She put her weight into him, but he pushed back. She flew over the back of the couch, landing on her feet, and he followed.

"Stop it! Get out of my house!" Adam screamed.

The assailant gave Adam a look that brooked no argument, but it was all the time that Alice needed. She jumped toward her purse and grabbed the knife out of the hairnet she kept there. She thrust forward and he dodged; her knife found the plush cushion of the couch. She blocked his underhand thrust with her left arm as she spun, and they began a dance. All of her brief training flooded back into her brain, but it was mostly defensive. She couldn't fight this boy that had been trained his whole life.

She did her best. She was panting and sweating, and Adam's living room wasn't in a condition to entertain anymore. Only one last touch would make it any worse.

CRASH!

He threw her bodily into the glass coffee table.

"Tommy, stop! You're going to kill her!"

Alice panted. She didn't feel keen on fighting back anymore, not with Tommy's knife at her throat. She stared at the teen, who smiled that sardonic smile back at her. The worst part was there was no malice in it. He looked almost proud as she felt the cold of the steel against her throat. He cocked his head as he looked deeper; looked into the fear that lit her eyes, the terrors that colored her past. Adam looked from one to the other. It was obvious Tommy wasn't trying to kill her, but that didn't make this okay.

They had ruined his living room, reminding him of exactly what Alice was. The lamp Alice had knocked over lay on the floor in its separate pieces, among a bit of blood that he was pretty sure belonged to Alice, though Tommy wasn't without his own scratches. No one moved, no one breathed, no one dared. The room belonged to Tommy.

Lightning fast, Alice's leg flew up as she attempted a move she had only seen once. To her surprise, it worked. Her legs were stronger than they had been, her body more agile. Tommy hadn't expected it, and now he was pinned to the floor. The knife flew out of his hands and skittered across the floor to join the broken lamp.

Tommy burst into laughter, pinned beneath Alice's leg.

Adam was only looking at Alice; besides scratches on her arms and back, she looked okay from her crash into the table. There was a cut on her forearm that didn't look so great, which must have been from the lamp.

Alice had forgotten he was even in the room. To her, the only thing there was Tommy. She stared at him, outraged at his laughter. "You can get off me now," Tommy chuckled. Alice climbed up and off him, limping on the ankle that she had hurt when she lost her own knife. "Good show!" Tommy laughed.

"What's wrong with you?" Alice screamed. Tommy looked up, innocently, infuriating her.

"I'm going to have a few bruises tomorrow, too, you know." Tommy said in defense.

"Tommy, I want you out of my house, now," Adam said, finally deciding to take charge of the situation.

"Chill out, ape. I'm paying you to let me be here."

Adam opened his mouth as if to say something before clenching it shut. The boy was right. No matter how much Adam hated it, this whole town was the Caraways' domain.

Tommy didn't take his eyes off Alice. "You're better than I thought you'd be. Where'd you learn fighting?" Tommy asked.

Alice said nothing. Her eyes were glassed over again and Adam saw it. He moved forward. He wanted to run to her side and put his hands on her shoulders, but she held up her hand, stopping him.

She looked back up at Tommy. "What *right* do you have to do this?"

"Well, I'm acting clan leader, don't you know." Adam choked in surprise and Tommy looked at him. Adam realized that he should have seen this coming: Finn never would have taken the responsibilities of the clan leader. "It's my job to get to know each and every one of my subjects," Tommy smiled before turning to Adam again, "You can feel free to treat her arm anytime, *Doctor*."

Adam gritted his teeth and found his bag under the table. Alice sat down hard in the armchair, her forearm bleeding everywhere. Adam dragged over an unbroken standing lamp and let it shine on the wound.

"This will need stitches."

"Well, get to it, why don't you?" Tommy said.

Adam took Alice by the elbow and led her to the bathroom so he could wash and sanitize the wound. She sat on the toilet, letting him take care of it, staring glassily into nothingness. He finished quickly and put his warm hand on hers.

"Alice, it's okay. You're here with me. He's not going to hurt you anymore." Her eyes looked down at him, though she refused to focus.

"I could have stopped him."

"Alice?" She didn't answer. "Alice, are you okay?"

She looked at him, "If I had believed in myself, if I'd have known, I could have saved her."

"Oh, Alice," he reached up and brushed her cheek. She held his hand there. "You can't change the past, sweetie."

She looked up. "But I can change the future," she smirked.

"OW!" Adam yelped, jerking his hand back. "Why did you do that?"

She eyed him, considering, "I'm sorry. It's become a habit when I'm deep in thought. I'm sorry, Adam."

"Yeah, it hurt," he said, cradling his shocked hand. "Why don't we just eat?"

She nodded placidly. There was something different. She wasn't lost in her netherworld; it was thoughts that had her occupied. He wasn't sure that he liked wherever her thoughts were leading her, at least not judging by the expression on her face. He led her out of the bathroom and down the hall to the kitchen. "Hey, you know, it wasn't your fault. You're only human…"

"No, she's not," Tommy said with his mouth full, sitting at the table, eating the dinner Adam had cooked for him and Alice. "I hope you don't mind, I took the liberty of serving myself," Tommy said casually. Adam's hands clenched into fists. "Don't look so bitter, doctor. I served you and Alice, too," he said, nonchalantly. Adam knew it was anything but nonchalant. Tommy loved pushing everyone's buttons, especially his, it seemed.

"Oh, and I think a New Year's party on your yacht is a great idea. I'd be happy to come." Adam's face went blank again as Alice looked up at him.

"I was going to invite you and your brother onto my yacht for New Year's." Adam said to the woman with the bandaged arm.

"Okay," she said, "The food smells good," Alice lit her face with an overused smile.

"Oh, don't worry, it is." Tommy added. Adam frowned but pulled a chair out for Alice and got the plates that Tommy had been so kind to set out for them. It might have been Tommy's way of apologizing for making a mess of his living room, or it could just be Tommy messing with his head. He never could tell with the boy. Alice sat smiling her distant, but ultimately false, smile. She moved mechanically bringing the food to her mouth, back to plate, and to her mouth again.

"It is very good," Alice said as Adam sat with his own plate.

"Thank you," Adam grumbled. The awkward silence spanned the length of dinner and only intensified when Tommy went up for seconds. Why couldn't the boy just leave? All that Adam had planned for the evening was falling to pieces because he was there. Adam had hoped to curl up on the couch and watch a movie with Alice, but that wasn't happening. As the silent dinner came to a close, Alice moved their dishes to the sink and threw her purse over her shoulders, ready to leave, lost in her own thoughts.

Tommy moved to the couch, turning on a sports channel. The TV had luckily escaped the massacre suffered by the rest of the living room.

Adam stepped into Alice's path, ignoring Tommy. "Would you like me to walk you home?"

She smiled at him, a real smile this time. "No thanks. I can make it home alone." She touched his hand briefly. Tommy was up in an instant and was suddenly beside the both of them.

"Well, if you're leaving, I'll go with you."

"I meant the whole 'alone' part," Alice said stiffly, this time.

"Well, we both know you can protect yourself," he smiled. She couldn't tell if he was being sincere or not. The current Alice so adored passed over her fingers once again.

"Now you're starting to get it," Tommy smiled, his sardonic nature showing only in his eyes.

Alice spun on him and shoved him into the door. Tommy laughed. "How the hell did you get to be this way?" Alice asked. Adam took a step back.

"We are all products of our upbringing, Alice," he laughed.

"Ugh. Do you ever give anyone a straight answer?"

Tommy stopped laughing. She jumped back as he reached out and shocked her. "No," he said bluntly. He looked at Alice's face and started laughing again. Alice might as well throw her

186

hands in the air. He wasn't a person you could deal with normally. She turned and found Adam right in front of her. He put his hands on her arms and she shook him off.

"Look, I'm going for a swim. Alone. You both can just leave me alone."

"Alice," Adam started.

"No, Adam, just don't. Thank you for dinner," She turned and found Tommy blocking her path this time. He smiled at her, his usual smirk this time.

"You mean you aren't going to thank me, too?"

"Get out of my way, Tommy."

"Oh, happily, my dear." He made a big show of stepping aside, bowing, and pushing the door open at the same time. Adam rolled his eyes.

"I hope you know you're an utter asshole," Alice told Tommy.

"Oh, I know," he said, giving her that sarcastic smile he had down to an art.

"Thanks again, Adam." With that, Alice stalked out, leaving the two men standing in the doorway. Adam spun on the boy.

"What game do you think you're playing?"

"Wouldn't you like to know, doctor."

"Don't you know she's…"

"Suffered some horrible tragedy in her past?" he paused, "Of course I do, Doctor Carson. But, my dear doctor, haven't we all?"

"You can't mess with people's lives like that!"

"Doc, we all manipulate those around us in one way or another. I just enjoy it."

"What were you really here for?"

"To enjoy your delicious food, of course, and destroy your living room," he said sarcastically. Adam was fully aware there was some truth to what Tommy said, only it was never the whole truth with Tommy, and his motives were a mystery. At least, his motives beyond the fact that Tommy obviously wanted to drive a wedge between him and Alice.

"Ugh. You really are a dick, Tommy. You really are."

"Yep, but I'm a dick who signs your paychecks. You'd do well to remember that." Tommy gave him a mock salute. "Cheerio, doctor." With that, Tommy finally left. Adam let out a sigh of relief. He thought of his dad. Leaving this town didn't sound like a very bad idea. Maybe his dad had it right, maybe dealing with the locals was a masochistic act akin to jumping off a boat with bricks attached to your feet. At least he knew Tommy would never do anything as blunt as that.

Alice stopped halfway to the beach, realizing it was the last place she truly wanted to be. For the past two days she had spent so much time with David, rekindling their sibling bond. She didn't want that right now; she wanted to be alone. She went home and borrowed the car instead. Driving out of Brassila Cove, she tried not to think of the woman it was named after. She drove just to be alone, just to drive, but found herself on some cliffs nearby. She stopped the car and got out, dangling her legs over the edge. She felt the ocean spray on her face as it beat against the cliff face. She remembered the air in Portland, the chillier ocean. She remembered standing in the ocean in California, watching her grandmother on the shore. Her life had always been tied to the ocean, even before she became a mermaid. Maybe she should have known.

She heard rocks crunching and turned around.

"Tommy." He smiled at her. "What are you doing here?"

"I followed you, of course."

"How the…?" She turned around and saw a Jeep next to her family's SUV. "Great," she said sarcastically, turning back to the water. Tommy nonchalantly joined her on the cliff. Briefly Alice thought about pushing him off, but it didn't make much sense. He'd live and she knew it; he was mer. Oddly enough, Tommy said nothing. He stared out at the ocean, then stared at her, but didn't deign to say anything, leaving Alice to her own thoughts. It almost reminded her of time with his brother.

Ironically, Tommy wasn't near as infuriating as his brother, despite what Tommy had just pulled that evening.

"I'm sorry 'bout scaring you earlier."

"No, you're not."

"No, not really. It was necessary."

"Why do you manipulate people like that?"

"I think it's fun."

"Even when it hurts people?"

"People take things too seriously." Alice thought about that for a moment, eyeing him sideways. "I don't care what happened in your past," he continued. "You have been given a gift and you just won't accept it. I'm only trying to help." He smiled the smile that turned her stomach.

Tommy paused as Alice eyed him up and down. She couldn't figure him out. Part of her believed him when he said that he was trying to help, but the way he said it nagged at her. It was the first time she had ever heard Tommy talk in a way that could be construed as sincere. Still, the expression on his face didn't make sense with the tone of his voice.

"Alice, if you don't like something, you have the whole of the ocean to escape to. You don't need to put up with anything: apes, or the folk, or me, or my brother. The ocean is yours. You have the perfect escape route. You don't need anything. What I don't get is why you're still here, pissing all manner of people off."

Alice looked back out at the ocean. It was truly beautiful. She smiled. Oddly enough, Tommy shared the smile with her. "Alice, you seem to keep forgetting that you're not a human anymore." Tommy let her mull that over as he got up and left as if he had never been there. He knew exactly where to nudge people, exactly when to be what kind of person. Exactly what buttons to push. He liked it that way.

Alice sat there a while longer. She couldn't leave the world she had known her entire life, could she? Her parents would be devastated. Or would they? She looked out at the ocean, still thinking like a human. She couldn't even begin to fathom the size of the ocean; she hadn't grown up there. She was still partly human, whatever Tommy said. She belonged to a human mother, a human father, and a human life. Or did she? What was there left of her human life when she became one of the mer? She felt almost as if her human life had ended the night she lie in the garage on the cold pavement, waiting for true death to take her; but it didn't. Hadn't she been a ghost since then?

She remembered that night in the ocean, the burn as her lungs filled with water, and the tug on her ankle. She remembered the feel of Finn's tail sliding across her legs, remembered the electric shock that sent her body into convulsions, but what she remembered most was the way she had given up. She looked up at the moon in the sky, got up, and left.

Chapter 16

New Year's

The waters shone sapphire in the fading sun, and the breeze that hit the five of them was refreshing, though the temperature was mild. New Year's Eve. Alice invited David, Tommy was there because he was Tommy and would never renege on a promise or a chance to mess with people, and somehow Alice found herself sitting next to the redhead they called the Selkie. Alice wasn't exactly sure why Kari was there, and the whole thing would have been highly awkward if she weren't drinking just a little bit.

Alice was reclining on the booth with Kari while she tried to figure out what kind of game the boys were playing on the other side of the boat. She tried to ignore Kari, but it was hard. Truth was, Kari seemed sweet and innocent, despite Alice's brush with her in the diner so long ago.

"I think they're playing chess," Kari said, breaking the long silence.

"What's David doing, then?" Alice wondered. Kari instantly looked down.

"I think he's watching," Kari answered. Alice looked at her. She couldn't get a proper read on Kari. She distrusted her, but she couldn't really stop the girl from hanging out with them. She just didn't understand why Kari would want to be with them when she had been party to the girl who had gone out of her way to threaten Alice.

"So what's your deal with Ashley?" Alice asked Kari suspiciously.

"Oh, Ashley," Kari said nonchalantly, watching the boys. "Ashley's just...well, she kinda adopted me when I came to live with this clan."

"Why do they call you Selkie?"

"I make my home in the waters off the coast of the U.K. We are called Selkies there because we wear the skins of seals to hide ourselves sometimes," she said, with a hint of nostalgia that made Alice curious.

"Why would you come out here if you loved it there?" Kari looked up, startled, not realizing her affection for her home had been so obvious.

Kari looked down. "All the men of the Selkies are mated," she said quietly. Alice looked away, feeling awkward for some reason. Kari fell silent. She didn't really speak much, and she didn't seem mean-spirited like Ashley, but she also didn't seem like the type who would ever be alone. She was short and small, which hid her age well.

"You aren't really after Finn?" Alice asked, the notion new to her.

Kari looked up startled. "Finn? Finn belongs to Ashley. She would never allow me to try to win Finn." Alice smiled. It was hard not to like the little redhead; she just seemed so sweet. Kari looked at Alice, emboldened by her smile, "Are you after Finn?"

Alice choked on some of her beer, "Hell, no."

"Tommy?"

Alice laughed. "I'm not after anyone."

"But you're…"

"I don't want anything to do with them." She looked at Tommy, wondered what it would be like, not for the first time, to just run off.

Kari put her hand gently on Alice's arm. "Then why are you here? I chose to come here. My clan was sad, but they knew: alone we are nothing. Only together can we achieve greatness."

Alice looked to the girl. She wasn't so little, she was of an age with Tommy and David, but it was hard to think of her that way. She looked almost as young as little Aria. She didn't want to break the girl's illusions, but Alice found it better to be alone. Somehow Kari sensed that.

"In our world, even the Wanderlusts pair off eventually," Kari said.

"Maybe I'm just not ready." Alice said, hoping to get off this topic. "Won't Ashley be unhappy you're hanging with us now?"

"Ashley does not own me. I am the daughter of the Selkies. I followed her before because her group was the only group of folk that were of an age with me, but she is not a good person." Alice was taken aback. There was more strength in her than she was wont to believe originally. It unnerved her.

"Is that why you've been hanging around? Or perhaps you're after the other Caraway?" Kari blushed.

"No," she said defensively. She smiled up at Alice sheepishly.

"Don't worry, your secrets safe with me," Alice said simply. "Come on, let's get the guys to dance." Alice got up and turned on the radio. She was pleasantly buzzed at that point and eager to get away from Kari.

"Come on guys! Let's celebrate." Alice said.

"Does there have to be dancing?" David asked.

"Oh, come on. Apparently it's what fish do on land, right, Tommy?" Alice said.

"Well, we could all break into a musical number, but I'm not sure the doctor would enjoy that." Tommy responded, "Checkmate."

"Yes, we can't forget the human can't breathe water," Adam laughed, knocking over the pieces. He moved to dance with Alice and Kari.

"What's that about, anyway?" David wondered. It was Kari

who answered him.

"When we sing, we sing of the joy of living in the water, of seeing wonders that they can't imagine. A human becomes dazzled and disoriented and will often try to drown themselves seeking that beauty and peace." Everyone looked at Kari. It was such a strange thing for her to say. For a moment, they all just stood there. Kari blushed openly.

"Well, now that that's settled," Alice took her brother by the hand and nearly spun him off the deck. Everyone laughed and the mood was lightened. They danced, all of them together, no partners, just fun, dancing, and drinking. It was peaceful; it was how life was supposed to go. Alice was genuinely enjoying the company as much as she could. It wasn't bad; Alice didn't feel her past weighing so strongly on her anymore. Still, she was much more comfortable when the festivities calmed.

It was after midnight. David and Kari were sleeping on opposite sides of the booth and Tommy had long ago receded back into the waters, to destinations unknown. Alice and Adam were sitting on the prow of the ship, their legs dangling over the side, passing the bottle of champagne back and forth as they watched fireworks in the distance.

"So, how do you like Brassila Cove now?" Adam asked slyly, passing her the bottle.

Alice looked back at her brother and the maid. "Not a shabby town you have here, doc. Strange, though. I think there's something in the water." She passed the bottle back. "Hey, how come you didn't visit your dad for the holiday?"

"Well, I'm going up to see him next week," he passed the bottle back.

"What happened to your mother?"

"Actually, my mom drowned, ironically."

"Ironic because you hang out with a bunch of fish?"

"Yeah, that would be it." They laughed quietly so as not to disturb the sleepers. Alice looked at him. She was seized with a sudden urge, part alcohol and part spontaneity. She leaned forward. He saw the gleam off her eyes and their lips connected. It was strange. Adam had hoped it would happen for some time now, but he was caught off guard. The strange buzz that numbed his lips tingled. She pulled away and he looked at her. She didn't look happy.

"What's wrong?"

"It's just, I..."

He touched her face. "It's okay Alice, I understand. You're not really ready for this."

"No, I'm not."

"It still cripples you, doesn't it?" Adam said, looking out at the sea, feeling about as awkward as he possibly could. "Your past."

"What do you know?" he heard an edge to her voice, the precursor to her closing off to him and everyone else around her.

"I know it hurts. More than you could express to any person on the planet, mer or human."

"Yes." The edge was gone. She relaxed, the tension released. It was odd, but he was glad she didn't try running away again.

"You know I'm here for you," Adam said. She looked up at him with sad little eyes.

"You're a really great friend," she said. His lips still tingled. He didn't want to just be her friend. Alice wanted to not be afraid, to not be cold, but it hadn't happened. Kari's story was getting to her; every mer needed a mate and she truly did care for Adam, but there was no spark. She enjoyed his company, enjoyed how he made her feel, and she could tell he wanted her, even if he was too honorable to pursue her. Part of her liked that about him. Maybe it was true, maybe she really wasn't ready. She couldn't get past the screams in her head. It hurt her that she couldn't, that she could seem so normal to everyone around her now and still be so very entrapped by her past.

She wondered to herself if it had destroyed her ability to feel anything for anyone. She looked back at David. No, she felt love and tenderness, and a dull ache for things to go back to the way they were before in Portland. Things would never be the same, though. She had grown, he had grown, and they were both part of a new world they hadn't even scratched the surface of, a secret that they had to keep from everyone else in their lives. Adam watched her mind spinning and spreading in all directions. It hurt him that she was cold, but he could understand it.

Alice turned back to him. "I just need more time," she said, sounding much more sure of herself than she really was.

"Alice, you can have all the time in the world." He put his arm around her in a friendly way, and she didn't move away. She was okay.

Tommy swirled into Ashley's company. She was stalking Finn again. She had a little cave that she liked to frequent where she could see Finn's every approach to 'his island.' Finn was spending almost all his time there now, and so Ashley was spending almost all her time in the cave.

"What do you want?" she asked fiercely.

"My favorite mad mermaid."

"If you weren't…"

"Oh, yes, you would rip my tail off my body, I know, my dear. I just thought you should know."

"Know what?"

"I spent the entire afternoon with the good doctor and your lovely rival."

Ashley moved back in the water, her tail flipping back and forth in irritation the way a cat's would. "She's not competition. She's falling for the doctor."

"Okay." He moved to swim away, a smile plastered to his face.

She spun around him, placing her knife to his chest. He pulled the short-sword at his waist and batted the knife away. It began to float downwards.

"What do you know, snake?" she hissed fiercely.

"Quite a bit, my dear," he said, replacing the sword. She glanced at it with narrowed eyes. It was the sword that should belong to the clan leader. She was sure when Finn stopped mourning he would reclaim the sword.

"What do you know?" she shouted and shoved him, sending her fierce shock waves through the water. Tommy smiled. He was playing with fire here, a fire that was completely insane; he could tell by the way her electricity varied in wavelengths.

"The doctor will never be enough for her, you know. She's in love with the ocean, dearie." He loved the look of shock on Ashley's face, the way the electricity streamed from her. He spun around, leaving the mer to her cave.

Tommy knew what he was doing, even if no one else did. Why should they? It was the way that Tommy played the game. Sooner or later he would have his checkmate and everything would turn out the way he had planned it. No one ever came to conclusions by themselves.

Chapter 17

Good Times

The next weeks passed in a blur, and soon it was almost February already. Alice was back almost completely. Her parents were beyond happy. Not only was their daughter there, but finally it seemed that even David was taking an interest in the town. Alice had introduced him to the younger Caraway and they were now great friends. Apparently Tommy had even taught David to surf. Of course, what their parents didn't know was that anytime they fell off their boards they went on a romp through the kelp and out further than their parents would have liked. As mer they were fast and sleek in the water, unstoppable.

Alice and Adam seemed to be an item to outsiders. Really, it was more like they circled around and around each other, never truly connecting. It was a strange dance. Adam felt for her more than he would say, but Alice just wasn't ready for that kind of relationship. Still, the Baileys couldn't have been happier. Alice often met Adam on his boat, but Adam couldn't join her in the water, not the way Alice swam. He felt it, too: it seemed the more time passed, the further she grew from him. He felt exactly how David had. He came up to a wall of glass every time he tried to touch Alice.

At the same time, Adam was teaching Alice to love the world again. He was showing her things in the world that were worth loving. Alice had loved the ocean first, and now Adam was teaching her to love other things, too. He was bringing her out, putting her back together, ever so slowly.

When Alice was in the ocean, the water filled and swirled around her heart, beating against the stones she carried inside. One day they were on his boat, just her, Adam, Tommy, and David. They were playing Twister, of all things. Adam and Alice were still on the mat. David was watching and laughing at them, and Tommy was spinning the spinner.

"Right hand blue."

"You know, I think you're cheating, Alice," Adam said.

"Why?"

"Well, I'm guessing you're not made up of the same thing as I am."

"You getting stiff, old man?"

"Don't call me old man!" he said, losing his footing and falling. "Dammit!" They all laughed.

"And the fish win at Twister!" David yelped. They all kicked back, grabbing beers from Adam's mini-fridge.

"So where's your brother, Tommy?" Adam asked.

"Why you ask?"

"Honestly, I thought I'd be stitching him up after some kind of fight after Brassila died."

"Nah, Finn knows how to take care of himself. I think he's avoiding the maids. Pretty sure they've redoubled their efforts, now that he's technically the clan leader. I heard a visiting maid got scratched up pretty bad the other week."

"She said she cut her hand cooking," Adam smiled.

"Must not have known we had a doctor on the payroll, then, eh?"

"You gonna pair off this year, Tom?"

"Aw, hell no. I'm trying to beat Finn's record."

"Finn still hasn't paired," Alice pointed out.

"Exactly," Tommy said, "Single as long as you can manage it. I thought you, of all people, would understand that, Alice." They all laughed, except Alice.

"Come on sis, it was just a jape."

"I know." The all heard a splash near the boat and looked over the side. There swam a red head that seemed to follow their group as often as Ashley followed Finn. Alice stood up and moved over to the rail.

"Kari, what's wrong?" Alice said after one look at her face. Kari grabbed onto the ladder and used her deceptively strong arms to climb up a couple of rungs, her tail still hanging in the water.

"Tommy," she breathed. She had swum at top speed to reach them. Tommy appeared behind Alice, along with David.

"The Marianas maid," she breathed, but Tommy already knew what had happened. He didn't need to hear another word. Adam appeared at the edge.

"Slow down, Kari," Adam said gently.

David took it upon himself to lift Kari up the rest of the way. The two of them fell on the deck exhausted. He wove out from underneath her while Adam got her a towel.

"Don't bother," Tommy said. "The Marianas maid is dead." Kari looked up at him, her big blue eyes full of terror. Adam turned to him from his place attending to Kari. David stood far away from everyone, and Alice hadn't moved at all.

"The one I…"

"No, it was the other visiting maid, the prettier one," Tommy said, his face all annoyance and seriousness.

Adam clenched his teeth, "Finn, I never…"

"It wasn't Finn." Tommy said, looking at Kari.

"Ashley," Kari said.

"Tommy, you're…"

"I'm not the clan leader. I can't do anything," he smiled. "Someone has to talk to my brother."

"I'll do it." David said. Everyone turned to him.

"You don't know my brother,"

"Tommy, why can't you just do it?" Adam asked, looking at a cut on Kari's wrist.

"My brother would have no qualms taking me down, at this point," he turned to look at Alice still hanging by the rail. All eyes followed his.

"Oh, hell no. How could you even...?"

"This is a serious problem, Alice. Who do you think she'll come after next?"

"Not me!" Tommy smiled that infuriating smile at her. "I'm pretty sure you're the only one who can, Alice." She scoffed.

"Fine, but you owe me." Alice pulled her shirt over her head and removed her pants. She didn't wear underwear anymore, but she was in the water before anyone could notice.

"Oh Alice, take this with you." She surfaced as Tommy tossed the short-sword into the water. It floated on the surface of the water for a few seconds before it started to sink Alice grabbed it and went off in the direction of his island. Tommy was right; she was the only one who could talk to that monster. She certainly wouldn't let David face him, and David was the only other person who understood exactly what Finn was mourning.

"Stop," Kari said to Adam. She moved to the edge of the deck.

"Where are you going?" David asked.

Kari turned, "If she's going to talk to Finn, I'm going to find Ashley. Maybe I can talk to her."

"You probably can't, you know," Tommy said.

"Someone has to try." Kari flipped herself backward over the edge of the boat.

Alice was in Finn's territory, but she saw no one on the island. She had almost turned around when she felt the blade against her throat. She was meters from the little island and his strong arms were around her. She felt the shock, she felt the knife, but it didn't scare her anymore. She shocked right back and spun around to face his perplexed blue eyes.

"What are you doing here? And why are you carrying that?" he pointed to the sword. Alice spun away from him and headed toward the island. It irritated him, the way she took the liberty of crawling onto its beach. He followed her all the same.

She pulled her tail up onto the beach and out of the water. He came up after her and she threw the sword at him. He dodged, but pulled it out of the surf before the waves could steal it. He looked down at it and looked at the matching emerald shining in her hair.

"Tommy sent you."

"Ashley's killed one of the visitors," Alice said

"What concern is that of mine? I gave this to Tommy."

"You are the clan leader! You need to do something about this."

"Actually, I've been considering leaving entirely."

"Yet you just can't leave your island," she said sarcastically.

"I would be well within my rights to execute you for encroaching on my territory."

"Yes, Tommy said you would do that if he showed up. Really, Finn? You'd kill your own brother, after losing your grandmother? Oddly enough, I didn't doubt you would."

He raised his eyebrows. "You've obviously met my brother," he paused, considering the maid, "You need to leave."

"You need to stand up for your own clan. You can't let her get away with this, Finn. I was there, I met your grandmother. You've been out here for months, living all by yourself. It doesn't work; trust me, I've tried." He looked up at her.

"I'm hiding from maids like you."

"Look, you arrogant brat, I'm not chasing you. I just want that clear."

"Oh, that's right, you have a human. You know, when you make it official, you'll be out of my ocean forever."

Alice was bristling. This was stupid. She was trying to help! She understood what Tommy was saying. Why couldn't Finn do anything about this? This woman was dangerous. Just because she cared about Tommy didn't mean she had to deal with this mess.

"Tommy's a much better leader than you."

"Perhaps he is. That's why I left him the sword." He tossed it back at her. She just stared at him, seething, bristling with electricity. She leapt into the water and disappeared. She swam back to shore. She wanted to be away for a while and, besides, she had work later. The tourists had begun coming in. They had to be more careful. They were required to use the private beach to disembark.

On her way out of what was well known as Finn's territory, a pair of eyes watched her and turned dark.

"Ashley," the mer spun to face the red-head.

"You," she narrowed her eyes, "how dare you return here?" Ashley pulled her knife from its place in a scabbard at her side.

"Ashley, please. I just came to talk."

"That's what you say. That's what they all say."

"I don't want Finn!"

Ashley moved close to the young mer who refused to draw her blade. "You follow the transform now."

"I don't follow anyone…" Ashley moved like a viper and there was blood in the water, Kari's hand flew up to stem the flow from her cheek. She stared at Ashley with wide eyes. One thing

Kari had never expected was that Ashley would kill her, but the look in her eyes brooked no argument: the intent was there, the intent to kill. Kari fumbled to draw her blade as the other mer came at her.

David crashed into Ashley at that exact moment. His blade was against the mer's throat, and Ashley's back was against the wall of her little cave. She had nowhere to go. She smiled evilly at the boy.

"She's not worth it," David slowly withdrew his knife and Ashley swam away, toward shore.

"Thank you," Kari said softly.

David turned and looked intently at the red-head, straight into her deep blue eyes.

Finn relaxed. He was back on his rock and the sun shone bright above and reflected off his scales, but Finn was lost in a world as gray as the one Alice knew so well. Finn was a leader now, a position he had never wanted. He knew he couldn't be single much longer, and yet he couldn't stand the company of anyone. He stared at the sword by the tree, in the spot where Alice had been sitting only moments ago. Brassila had known instinctively how to lead. Finn knew nothing but his own world, and the fact that he did not want to lead. He couldn't stand the thought of being in charge.

"You're an idiot, Finn." Finn turned suddenly. Tommy had surfaced not too far away.

"Tommy, you know the rules. You have no excuse to be here."

"No reason, except to call you an idiot," Tommy said with his characteristic sarcasm.

"What do you want, Tommy?"

"Finn, you been like this since mom died. Get over it. Both mom and grandma would call you an idiot. Since they're not here, I'm doing it for them. Grow up, Finn."

"Brassila would never call me an idiot."

"Nope, but she'd be thinking it." Finn gave him an irritated predatory look. If it were another of the folk they would have left in an instant, terror in their eyes. Tommy just sneered at him and disappeared under the waves. Grudgingly, Finn slipped into the water and started swimming toward the shore. It was better when he slept in a locked house where no one could bother him, except, of course, Tommy. He was tired of the beach anyway.

They just wouldn't let him be. The maids had redoubled their efforts. They knew very well that no mer had ever led a clan by himself. This murder; he knew it was because of him. The other clans heard things. Wanderlusts were known to come in and out, they would spread all kinds of news over what was left of their ocean.

Brassila had led alone after the death of his parents. Then again, his grandmother was unlike anyone he had ever met. She was strong, capable, and independent. They didn't make people like that anymore, and it had always been a rare trait. The women chasing him wanted the power he symbolized without any of the drawbacks that went with it, and he knew that Ashley would stop at nothing to be with him. That didn't mean she was his problem. Let her mate with Tommy instead.

Sooner or later he would be forced to mate, but he wanted it to be his choice, and he certainly didn't want a vindictive, murderous maid. But he wasn't about to deal with her, either. She wasn't his problem. He had named Tommy the leader, but Tommy had the gall not to tell anyone. Until the point where they forced him, though, he thought he would enjoy his last moments of freedom.

Chapter 18

Tom Sawyer

Alice swam hard and fast and straight for shore. Her muscles ached from the effort, she still hadn't developed a speed that matched those born mer. She wanted to burst into tears, but she didn't know why. She disembarked, only to find Ashley there. Alice looked up at the maid, who stared straight back at her.

"How are things with Adam?" she asked, sickly sweet.

"Things are fine," Alice said, grabbing a towel of her own to dry off with.

"I'm glad. I feel I haven't been very hospitable to you lately. I thought we could go for a swim tomorrow," she said.

"Thanks for the offer, but I have work."

"Enjoy!" she said as Alice's legs returned to her. Alice got up as quick as she could and left Ashley there.

Ashley knew she was chasing Finn. The thing with the doctor was only a cover. She would have to be sure first, but sooner or later, she would take her rival down. She decided to stalk Alice instead of Finn, just looking for her moment. It wasn't a long time coming. After only took two days of following her, Ashley found exactly what she was looking for.

Alice stalked into the house, in full view of the windows of the ballroom, where Ashley could see her perfectly. She wasn't even trying to hide. Finn was walking down the steps. He saw Alice and began to flee. At least he was doing that right. Fleeing the transform was exactly what he should do. Alice was playing him for a fool, just like she thought she was playing Ashley. But Ashley wouldn't be fooled; Tommy had confirmed her fears. The sneaky little bitch was going to have to go down. It had started when she stole the Selkie, the little redheaded girl who thought she could come back and spy on Ashley. Ashley had shown her what was what, leaving a mark across her cheek, just as she had the North Pacific girl's hand. The North Pacificker had been quick to flee when Ashley took down the Marianas girl, who had thought she could sneak past Ashley's defenses. Ever since the slap in her face when Alice did her little make-over trick, Ashley had known it would come down to this. How dare the transform take the gift of the hairnet-knife that was meant to be hers.

"Finn."

Finn started walking the other direction, hoping she would just go away.

"Finn!"

He quickened his pace. As soon as he reached a room he

could lock the door in her face.

"Finn, stop." Alice grabbed his wrist. He spun to see her angry face. Oddly, seeing her angry made him less angry. "I was just going to ask you where your brother was. He was supposed to meet me and David."

"Do I look like my brother's keeper?" Finn asked coldly.

"No, but you're supposed to be the clan leader. I thought you might know where your people were," Alice snipped.

He pulled his wrist out of her hand, almost surprised to find it was still there. "I told you, I don't, and never did, want to be clan leader."

"Too bad for you, you are. Someone once told me you have to deal with the hand you're dealt."

"That person was either an idiot or a certain doctor that pokes his head in places it doesn't belong." She stared at him fiercely, then stalked away, headed for the ocean. Ashley had already slipped back into the waves.

"That sounded fun." Alice spun to see who had been talking. Leaning against the wall stood Tommy, complete with a smirk on his face.

"Where the hell were you?"

"Don't snip at me princess."

"You're such a dick sometimes, Tommy."

"And you all love me for it, so why should I stop?" He ran past her and leapt to the waves, dropping his pants on the way there. Alice grudgingly followed. They met David and went to play under the waves, but Alice wasn't really into it. She was busy looking forward to another dinner with Adam. As she left the boys to return to shore early, Tommy watched her go.

Alice sat on the shore drying herself off. The scales were almost gone when someone else emerged from the water.

"You need to leave now, half-breed." Alice looked up. It was Ashley. Her eyes were wild, her hair plastered against her face. "You've worn out your welcome ten times over."

"What do you want, Ashley?" Alice said calmly.

"You think you have the others fooled: you and the doctor. I know better. You're trying to throw everyone off. You're after Finn just as much as the rest of us."

Alice laughed, "You're crazy." Suddenly, Ashley was on top of her, a knife at her throat. Alice stopped short and didn't breathe. She was afraid of Ashley. With the look in Ashley's eyes, she would be crazy not to be afraid.

"You'll fight me here. Tomorrow. On land. Or you will never touch the water again." Ashley said acidly.

"I don't want to fight you, Ashley," Alice said, trying to keep her voice calm and steady.

"You'll make your choice tomorrow. If you are not after Finn, you are with the doctor, and if you're with the doctor, you have no right to be in my ocean." Ashley withdrew her knife, then rolled over and let Alice up. Alice leapt to her newly-formed feet and ran. She saw the look in those eyes. She had been a bug under Ashley's heel. It was a threat, and not one to take lightly.

Alice blew into Adam's house the instant he opened the door. The delicious smells of dinner lit the air, but it didn't mean anything. Alice had seen what Ashley had done to Kari, and Kari hadn't dared to go into the water since; she was laid up in a room in the mansion, hiding from Ashley. Tommy was protecting her until Finn had some big epiphany and decided to take on his responsibilities. Alice had no faith in that ever happening and she had to deal with the cards that were on the table.

"Alice? You're a little early." Adam said, surprised at her disheveled appearance. It was obvious Alice had come there directly from swimming. He had expected her to get a little more ready than bikini and wrap.

"You were right you were right about everything. I should have listened. Ashley challenged me to a fight." Adam had a horribly stupid look plastered to his face as she looked to him for guidance. He sat down helplessly. "I don't want to fight her, but she threatened me. It doesn't seem like something I can get out of. Tomorrow morning. On land."

"She's giving you a chance, fighting on land," he said, waking up, "In the water she'd overtake you in seconds. She's trained all her life." His voice was empty. He was keeping it level, but he was afraid.

"I don't care what kind of chance she's giving me. I don't care about Finn! Is there any way out of this?"

Adam looked at her, his eyes as empty as his voice. "The only way out would be if Finn interfered." Adam knew better than anyone else that Finn wasn't about to interfere.

"I don't think I'm fighting just for Finn. I have a feeling Ashley wants me to give up the ocean entirely."

"So just do it." Adam said, throwing his arms around her. She was stiff but she looked up at him. He pinned a kiss to her and was answered with cold, unresponsive lips. "Stay with me! Go public with me. I love you, Alice." She stayed there a moment, pausing in the warmth of his arms, letting him comfort her.

Alice suddenly pushed him away, almost enraged, though she didn't shock him. "Adam, I care about you. I'm just not ready to give up the ocean for you. The ocean is the only place I feel like a person."

He slumped against a table, then looked up at her. She was so distant from him now. He felt like he was grasping at a bar of soap that he had neglectfully dropped into the ocean. Trying to catch a fish with bare hands. "Alice," he breathed.

"I do care about you. I just...I can't right now." She turned; she was leaving. There were tears in her eyes. She had let this go too far. This wasn't it. She couldn't lose the ocean, but Adam was the person who had been there for her from the very beginning.

"Alice, you can't do this," he said, scrambling to his feet. "I can't stitch you up when you come back in pieces."

She paused at the door, "Then don't."

She'd said it to be mean; she felt horrible, but she just had to think. She hadn't gone back to meet him for dinner at his house. She didn't really feel like eating anything. She had gone for help and all he did was throw himself at her, throw his love in her face, a love Alice knew full well about, but couldn't even begin to reciprocate. Instead, she headed the one place that had been home to her for so many terrible nights.

She walked through the gaudy pineapple and set her money on the bar. One way or another, Alice didn't think she would need it for anything but booze.

"Haven't seen you in a while," the bartender said.

"Look, I don't need your judgments. Just keep the booze coming." She took the shot of Jack that was the first thing offered, then grabbed the beer next to it. She quickly moved to her spot near the wall. Jaeger, Jack, and a few beers later she sat, staring out at the ocean, contemplating. She could hear the song of the waves and all the creatures in it while her head spun.

Who said she had to decide her whole life right then? Whose crazy idea was it? She could stay with Adam. It would take time, but she knew she could be a whole person again. She just couldn't contemplate giving up the ocean. Why would she have to? To never enter that kingdom again, to never be truly at peace: that would be pure torture.

David knew about the scheduled duel now, most likely from Tommy. He told her she should just run away, but he couldn't do anything. He couldn't make it better, whatever she did. She was on her own and it was her decision. She could throw down her knife and refuse to fight, but she couldn't go in the ocean again if she did: Ashley would make sure of it. With no one opposing her, there was no way to say she couldn't.

Why'd they even come to this stupid town? What would Grandma Emma have decided? She had decided: Emma had given up the ocean. Alice wondered, if Emma had the chance to do it again, whether she would have made the same decision. Alice remembered that look of longing in her eyes. Would that happen to Alice, too? Would she become an old woman watching her grandchildren playing in the surf, longing to join them? She put her head in her hands. She never wanted any of this.

Adam entered the mansion, turning the key that he still had from when he had to check on Brassila all hours of the night. He went straight to Finn's room. Finn was there, hiding from the world, no doubt. Luckily, Adam had a key to that closet-sized room, too. He opened the door and looked at Finn in the single bed crushed against the wall. He was wound up so tightly in the sheets that it had to be almost suffocating. That was the way the folk were: more comfortable when they had something wound around them, like the ocean. Adam grabbed Finn's feet and yanked the small-framed man out of the bed. Finn woke up before he hit the floor.

"You bastard!" Adam screamed.

"What?" Finn was sitting up, glaring at Adam with the shimmer to his eye that allowed him to see in the dark. He gingerly began to unwind himself from the sheets.

"You have to stop this!"

"Stop what?" Finn asked poisonously, losing patience fast.

"Ashley. You're the leader. You're the only one who can stop her."

"I never asked to be a leader, Adam, you know that. I believe I've turned down the job multiple times. I don't interfere in the affairs of others."

"Ashley will kill Alice whether or not she lays down her weapon. You know that."

"What's that got to do with me?"

"She's your clan!"

"You love her, stop her."

"You are such a brat. Brassila never would have let this madness continue."

"I'm not Brassila."

"No, Finn. You're nothing like your grandmother."

Finn's eyes narrowed further than Adam had ever seen before. "Leave now, Mr. Carson." It was an order impossible to refuse and Adam left stymied.

Finn crawled back into bed, but he couldn't sleep. He kept seeing the demons that haunted him. Finn had been in charge once. He had done the worst he could have. He couldn't be responsible. He couldn't handle it. He didn't want any more blood on his hands.

Chapter 19

Sea Witch

It was 4:45. Alice was already up.

"Alice, don't," David said from his doorway. He couldn't do anything about it. She looked at him.

"Don't worry, Dave." She took his hand and squeezed it. "I won't." Her eyes were filled with sadness, the weight of her decision on her shoulders. She walked into the lightening world outside, knife clutched close to her chest. She didn't even bother to stop him when she knew David was following. He kept his distance. He knew she had to face this alone. Alice wanted to cry but she wouldn't. She could smell the ocean, then let it surrounded her.

Ashley was waiting for her on the cold sands of the private beach, smiling. Alice walked straight up to her and dropped the knife on the sand at her feet. "You win, witch," she said. She turned to walk away when she heard Ashley's maniacal laugh from behind her.

"You think that's enough? You think I'll just let you go?"

"I submitted to you! You won! What else do you want?"

"You challenged me." Ashley said simply. "You challenged

me in every sense of the word. You don't get to just walk away." Alice stared, horrified, as Ashley picked up the other knife. Now she was armed with both of them. "You've been a thorn in my side since you came to town. You aren't walking away from this."

Ashley lunged. A bright red stripe appeared across Alice's arm before she could dodge. She was on the ground, scrambling to her feet to avoid the crazed maid.

This was insane! Alice dodged blow after blow, but she knew she couldn't keep it up forever. She knew the laws now. One of the folk had filled her in on what she needed to know. The challenge had been made and, by some weird logic, Alice couldn't get away from it. The only person who could truly interfere would be the clan leader, Finn. Finn, king of dispassion and apathy. She looked up at David. He was far away. He looked like he was going to run and interfere, but Zita came out of nowhere and held him with her strong arms.

He struggled but he couldn't get away. No, this was Alice's fight. It wasn't much of a fight. Ashley was armed with both weapons and all Alice could do was dodge blow after blow. She was doing remarkably well so far, but she knew she couldn't keep it up forever. Ashley was already pushing her toward the ocean. They both knew that Ashley had the upper hand there. The only thing Alice had going for her was those long-ago self-defense lessons. Dodge, block, dodge, block, another red stripe and a cry of pain. This couldn't go on forever.

"Why don't we open up that scar again? See if we can't get it just a little deeper," Ashley smiled, staring at the scar on Alice's side. It was hopeless. She wished Adam was there, but at the same time she didn't want him there, didn't want to him to see her fall.

Finn was watching with disinterest as Alice avoided the crazy girl.

"You could stop this." Tommy said, coming downstairs.

"There's no way to stop a maid like that. She will continue till her challenger is dead." Finn responded. "That maid is insane."

They were in the surf now, almost waist deep, Ashley gradually moving Alice toward the open sea.

"I can see a way."

"Is it a chess game to you?" Finn said.

Tommy looked up at his brother. "It's always a chess game with women. Ashley's not just challenging Alice; she's challenging your authority. She knows you won't stop it. She wouldn't listen if you tried. She's a beautiful woman."

"Ashley?" Finn raised an eyebrow.

"Alice."

Finn looked back at his brother, and Tommy stared right back at him with that smirk of his. Tommy knew. Tommy had engineered the entire thing, and that wasn't what Finn was thinking about. Finn remembered the current that ran through him when Brassila had been holding both his hand and Alice's. The way

225

Brassila smiled at him. That knowing smile, with just a hint of sarcasm; the same sarcasm that ran in Tommy's blood in excess. In the next moment, in his mind's eye, he was holding Alice in his arms, his knife pressed to her throat and his eyes widened.

"Your past makes you blind, Finn."

Finn looked back at the fight. Ashley had her. If Alice fell, she would turn. If Alice fell, Ashley would kill her. There was only one way he could stop it; he saw it just as Tommy already had. Ashley's back was to him, but he knew the kill lust in her eyes. He did not want to get between a crazed maid and her target. "You knew all along,"

"Saw it from the very start." Tommy smiled at the fight.

Finn looked at Tommy. "I hate you, Tom."

"Back at you, Finn."

Finn burst from the door. He was a shot across the beach, stripping off his shirt as he ran. No time for the pants; he would just have to let them rip when his tail appeared.

Impact! Finn hit Alice full force. He felt a stripe of pain open across his back as Ashley's blow hit him instead of her intended target. His arms were around Alice, his lips pressed against hers as they fell into the deep.

Alice was awash with a sensation she had never felt before. It wasn't something she could describe. It was electricity, it was chemical. But she knew and he knew and it just didn't make sense.

Her tail was around him before she could even process what was happening; her cuts burned in the saltwater but she didn't feel them. She just felt him; felt the warmth from his kiss. Like nothing on earth.

Then, so many images flashed through her brain at lightning speed that she could hardly separate one from the other. She knew him; she knew everything about him; she knew his soul because it was the other half of hers. She saw things she couldn't understand and things she could: they were his memories, his experiences.

Finn disentangled himself from Alice. He didn't need to continue the kiss. He knew so much about her already, and had for a while. He just hadn't wanted to see it, didn't want to be a part of it. He knew exactly what Tommy had already seen.

Chapter 20

Checkmate

Ashley looked down at the water. She couldn't contain her anger. The water was too disturbed: she couldn't see anything. She wouldn't go down, not with Finn down there. Finn was born a folk; he knew the arts even better than she. She knew, like all the true folk knew, that Finn's knife had been stained with blood before.

Finn had a blade, though not the short-sword left on his island. He pushed Alice away and down. He was shooting at top speed towards the surface, toward the blurry figure above the water. He was out and Ashley knew the look in his eyes.

"No," she breathed. Finn's knife made one slice and the slash appeared across her neck, blood poured into the water. Ashley reached up, sputtering, as Finn came down, as Ashley fell. He was already dragging Alice out of the water as Ashley faded into the surf. Alice was watching in horror from Finn's lap, his strong arms wrapped around her. It was so warm, yet she didn't dare look at him. Her tail flopped in the surf.

"Alice!" David was running toward his sister. In her horror, Zita had released him. Zita was now running toward the water and disappearing into it. Alice was just so confused; her head was swimming with all she had seen, with all she knew.

Finn lifted Alice up to her brother, who dragged her further up the beach. Tommy was calmly walking toward Finn, helping him out of the water as well. "Good job, Finn," Tommy said, as if what had just happened were nothing.

"I hate you," Finn spat.

"It's only because I was right."

Finn looked down at Alice. Alice was not looking at him, but David was. He looked terrified, and Finn didn't blame him. David had seen the way Finn dispatched Ashley; it was a heck of a way to meet Finn, from David's point of view. Finn had never even bothered to introduce himself to the new transform.

David didn't know what had just happened. Suddenly Finn knew his sister better than he did; just as Alice knew Finn better than anyone on the planet. Alice had seen that moment, as if it was her own memory, when Finn had first spilled blood. She knew how much it had destroyed him.

He couldn't have been more than eleven when his mother died, but it wasn't a boating accident. One of the doctors who knew the secret had gone rogue. Most would sell an arm or leg to study the folk: this man had sold his soul. He had drugged Finn's mother, followed her out to sea, and then tried to capture her, alive. His mother had known and she struggled for all she was worth. The doctor ended up accidentally stabbing her with her own blade. She had died. There had been so much water in the boat that she had dissolved right there. She had melted in the horrible man's arms, and he had flicked the remains away like they were something disgusting.

Finn had seen the entire thing. He knew the doctor wouldn't stop, and the man knew the woman had family. Tommy had been only three at the time. He would have been easy prey, along with Finn's father, who had gone completely insane when his mate had died. So Finn did what he had to do, but he did more than that. Finn had butchered the man, tortured him. The man had to pay for destroying his mother, for destroying his family.

She heard the man's laugh in her head, just as Finn had heard it then. She knew, just as Finn had realized at the time, that he had become the monster he hated. Finn never would let himself be in charge of anything after that. Tommy knew what had happened, but he didn't know what Finn had done, beyond eliminating the threat. Finn didn't hate the world; he hated that he saw that evil in himself.

She wouldn't, couldn't look at him. Not then. She needed air.

"Come on, Finn, let's get you to the good doctor. That cut looks bad," Tommy said as Finn's tail disappeared. Tommy handed his brother a pair of drawstring shorts, and Finn winced as he slipped them on. Finn didn't stop looking at Alice as Tommy led him away. Alice avoided his eyes the entire time.

"Alice, are you okay?" David asked.

Alice looked up at him with tears in her eyes, but they weren't hers. They were tears for Finn. "Please," she said, "Don't ask. Just let me go."

David released her and she clambered toward the ocean; the ocean, the only thing that made any sense right now. She disappeared beneath the waves and let herself go. David stepped forward.

"I wouldn't," Tommy said gently. Finn leaned heavily on his shoulder, paying attention only to the disappearing tail.

David turned to Tommy, watched the blood from Finn's back gradually crawl down to fall in the sand. Tommy seemed the only person aware of what was going on.

"She needs me."

"I'm pretty sure she needs quiet. She seems the type. However, I could use your help with this dead weight." Tommy motioned toward his brother. It was all Finn could do to remain on his unsteady legs.

David turned back toward the ocean. She could be anywhere by now, somehow, though, he knew he could find her.

"If you're good I might even explain some of what happened," Tommy smiled.

David sighed and turned his back on the water. He moved underneath Finn's other shoulder. Finn stared at David, as if just realizing the two of them existed. With David's help they were going to make much better time. Perhaps they might even make it to Adam's before anyone noticed the party.

"You told me," David grunted.

"Your sister and my brother are one and the same now." Tommy smiled at David smugly. The expression made David want to punch him in the face; with Finn's eyes fluttering it was impossible to do so. David knew by the expression and the smile that lit Tommy's eyes: all of this had been his plan from the beginning. Maybe they were destined for each other it—wasn't something David could begin to understand—but the fight and the dramatic rescue by Finn was all engineered and executed all by Finn's younger brother.

"You planned this," David said, gritting his teeth instead of punching him.

"Of course."

Chapter 21

Great Vacation

Alice was tired. She couldn't swim anymore and she couldn't fight the current, so she drifted and soon found herself crashed against a rock. She clung to the surface with all the strength she had in her. It took her a few moments before she realized she was sobbing, and she didn't even know remotely where she was. She pulled herself higher on the rock, letting the waves shower her with foam. She didn't even know who she was anymore. There were so many things swimming in her head, images and memories that didn't have anything to do with her.

The head of a seal poked out of the water. It looked at Alice, clinging to the rock like it was the only thing keeping her alive. As the seal climbed out of the water, the tail was longer than any seal's. Curious, Alice looked up.

Kari threw the head of the sealskin back. Alice blinked at the redhead in surprise. "What?"

"My tribe often wears sealskins. It is one of the ways we go unnoticed among the North Atlantic waters. It's why Ashley called me the Selkie."

"Why are you here?"

"For you." Alice glared at her. "You mated with Finn."

"I don't know what just happened." Alice said, staring at her unstable reflection in the water.

"You were not born of us; how could you?" Kari brushed a lock of Alice's hair from her bright green eyes. Alice looked at the girl. Her smile was as disarming as one of Adam's, if not more so. "It is different for a human," she looked at Alice's eyes, "This rock, it can live apart from every other rock for all its life, and never know the difference, yet with another rock it can build an island, a shoreline. To the rock it does not matter what other rock it finds, but together they can build something greater. Alone it is still a rock for you to cling to."

The tears stopped as Alice looked at the young mer, although at the moment she didn't seem near as young as she looked.

"That is what life is for a human. They can be alone or together. For us, it is different. We are built in halves." She smiled, sitting up. "Half land, half sea. Half human, half fish. Half in, half out. And half of each other. If you pull a plant from the dirt, it will die. Only planted in soil with the right nutrients will it grow. If you break a twig in half, it will only fit back together one way. We are each half a twig. Only when we find our other half can we grow."

Alice opened her mouth to say something, to deny something, to make some argument. How was it possible that his memories swam through her brain? Anything to make sense of this madness. She found Kari's finger to her lips.

"Alice, you are not human anymore. I once said it had to be hard for you. This is just one way. Had you remained only what you were, maybe you could have found happiness with the doctor, maybe you would have wandered the globe like we do when we cannot find our other half and ended up settling for something. You are of the folk now."

"Adam…"

"Should have known better than to get emotionally involved."

"How can you say that? It's not his fault!"

"It is, Alice. That's what you don't understand. He knew full well what we are, even if you didn't." Alice looked at Kari again. There were necklaces around her neck, beautiful things engraved with Celtic designs. The skin perched around her shoulders; it seemed so much emptier than it had when she swam up, almost as if when she was in the skin it was a live seal.

"Where are you going?" Alice couldn't tell how she knew, she just knew. Kari smiled at her.

"There is something I must do at home before I mate. After I kiss him, it will be too difficult to be such a great distance from him."

Alice looked at the water, "Tommy." Kari blushed and looked away, shaking her head slightly.

"What about you, what will you do?" Kari said, abruptly

shifting the subject away from her.

Alice looked out into the distance, closing her eyes against the spray falling against her face. "We have to go."

"You sense him."

"Yes." She looked at Kari. "It's so weird." Kari laughed, the ringing of her voice echoing off the cliff face, making even Alice smile. Kari returned her smile.

"Well what are you waiting for? Go to him!"

"No," Alice frowned. Kari looked confused.

"There is someone I have to say goodbye to first."

"Alice, he will get over you. He knew from the start." Alice smiled a sad little smile at the small mer. She would never call her young again.

"Like you said, I'm half human," Alice shrugged. Kari nodded as Alice slipped off the lonely rock and into the water.

Alice found Adam sitting on the wall behind the bar. She quietly joined him, but didn't say anything. Adam knew. Alice knew that Adam knew.

"I seem to remember a time when you were drunk up here," he said bitterly.

"Which time?" He didn't even look at her. "Perhaps they should post a sign: No drunks on the wall." Alice said.

"Or maybe a sign coming into town: 'Beware Sirens Afoot.'" He took a swig of his drink. "You know, when I went back to visit my dad, he chased me out of the house when I mentioned how I felt for you, one of the fish."

"I didn't know," she said softly.

"You certainly are two of a kind. A pair of the most mentally fucked up people I've ever seen. The worst part," he said, gesturing with his beer, "is that some part of me knew all along."

"I could have never been your woman."

"Don't give me that 'you weren't good enough for me' crap."

"I didn't mean for any of this to happen."

"No, it was that dick, Tommy. Manipulated the whole buggered thing."

"Tommy?"

"You better believe it, asshole," he added as an aside. They sat silent for a few moments; Alice was on the verge of tears. She loved Adam; she didn't want him to hurt like he did. At the same time, she could never be with him, even before everything had happened with Finn. He was right: she was all sorts of fucked up, and the only one who could understand was the one person she had never wanted anything to do with. It wasn't love as a human saw it; it was something different, something more. Finn was her match, her destiny. Some part of her hated it, hated that the decision was out of her hands. Her love for Finn was born in an instant, though Adam had worked for his place in her heart.

"I just..." her voice choked.

"You're part of the ocean. I never really could have asked you to give up the ocean. If I had taken it from you, I would have been kicking myself all my life. It never would have worked," he said, smiling faintly, grabbing her hand and squeezing. "It's not your fault. I just could never understand it like you do." The tears were streaming from her eyes now as the sun set behind them. He put his arm around her and held her close while she cried. It meant nothing anymore. She was beyond his reach. He could only hope she'd retain a piece of him. "I would have hated myself for taking you from the water." Alice couldn't answer. It hurt; it hurt in a wholly different way than her pain from before. Adam knew he would heal, he knew it was coming; he knew he couldn't have her.

"It's okay, Alice, I understand," he said, pulling her hair from the tears on her face. She composed herself, cried a little less. He wondered how hard it really was to suddenly have feelings for someone where there weren't any before, to know things about someone that they didn't understand themselves. He wondered if he could survive the process, had it been reversed. Then again, Adam always knew that Alice was stronger than she thought she was. It seemed to him he had always been the only one who knew, but he wasn't after all.

"You think anyone will notice Ashley's gone?" she asked as

he stared at the ocean and the last bit of disappearing sun.

"Ha," he said, "People disappear and appear here so often, no one will think anything of it." He gave her a sidelong glance. "People will notice when you're gone."

She nodded. "Everything's just so fresh. I have to get away." She didn't bother asking how he knew. Adam had always been perceptive; he wasn't an idiot, that was for sure. She didn't have to say she was leaving; she didn't have to admit it was with Finn. He knew. Finn and Alice were cut from the same cloth. Tommy would be in charge for a while, but now he knew Finn would find his way back eventually. Then everything would be different. Perhaps it was time that Adam thought about leaving himself.

"What are you going to tell your parents?"

She smiled softly. "You think Mom will complain if I say I eloped with the local millionaire?"

He smiled back. "She'll be heartbroken that she doesn't get to fuss over you in a wedding dress." They laughed a small, awkward laugh. "You know, at some point I would have put money on the mermaid side of your family being you mom's side. Your Dad, the dentist...he just doesn't strike me as very fishy." She laughed a real laugh, and he relished in the sound. There was something magical about the folk, even when they broke your heart. They sat for a while longer; Adam's beer was half-finished. She took it from him and took a huge swig.

"I have to go write my parents an important note." Alice said. He smiled at her; a strong, winning smile, the same one she had seen when she first met him. She had been much more broken then. Now she knew she had a home, and she was needed. She was climbing off the wall, on her way away. Adam was going to just let her go when a thought struck his mind.

"Hey, Alice."

She turned her green eyes back on him. "Yes?"

"Promise me something."

"Anything."

"Don't come back without a little fish." She smiled back at him, the sweet broken one. He knew it would brighten up soon enough. When Alice came back, she would be completely different. Would he even recognize her? He had to shrug it off; he couldn't dwell on anything. "Any kid the two of you have is bound to be adorable," he continued. Alice's smile grew stronger.

"I promise."

David and Alice stood on the private beach, early the next morning.

"Do you have to go?" he asked.

"I do. I couldn't describe half of it to you, little brother." She paused, staring at the ocean, the ocean that meant so much to her.

"You'd be surprised what I understand," he muttered, thinking of a bright pair of blue eyes. Alice turned on him.

"Really?" He nodded and she punched him in the shoulder. They laughed together for a moment, brother and sister. "You think mom and dad will ever forgive me?" Alice wondered.

"About a minute after you come back. You are coming back, aren't you?"

She grabbed him and gave him a hug. "I promise I'll come back. You gonna be alright?"

"Hey, me and Tommy are great pals, dick that he is. We'll be fine without you. Now, are we going for a romp through the kelp or what?" She smiled at him and leapt into the water.

They swam together for a while, singing to each other songs of play, songs of childhood. There were no words; it was all emotion. Then another song joined them. It was distant, but Alice recognized it immediately. Brother and sister stopped in the water. Alice looked to David.

"Well, go after him, then."

She could see him in the distance. He was there, waiting for her, singing her song, happy with an ever fainter tint of sadness.

She raced toward him, leaving David behind. Finn raced forward. They raced each other to *their* island. He leapt from the water to the small beach. She was behind him. Alice was staring at the mark on his back, stitched up so neatly. Gently, ever-so-lightly, she traced it. He looked at her; there was fear in his eyes. It was a strange feeling, knowing a person that well. Both had moments in their past they didn't want to share, yet knowing that the other knew was a relief, a burden that was no longer on their shoulders.

He grabbed her wrist. She looked up at him with terrified eyes as he placed her hand against his cheek. He was over her now. He touched the scar the mugger's knife had made in her side. She flinched, but didn't stop him. Their tails were out of the water, the sun was high in the sky. His strong hand traveled up her side as he leaned in to tenderly kiss her lips. A soft current ran through both of them. Their tails were gone, and her legs wrapped around him. His slight frame was wound in her arms. His strength was with her. Her strength was with him. He was with her. The ocean was inside her as they danced together. Her inner scars disappeared with his. The world was okay, and brightening by the moment.

They lay together all day and watched the red sun set. She hoped that Adam would be on his boat tomorrow, enjoying the sea the only way he knew how. Finn leapt into the water and she leapt after him. They set out, not to learn about each other, but to learn the world, and how to be happy now that they knew each other. Their song had such a slight hint of sadness that you would hardly know the horrors they had seen.

They danced together in the water with the multitude of life around them, following the setting sun.

Afterward

I suppose I could begin by thanking everyone who helped me get this here. Truth be told, I don't even think it's done, but to a writer nothing is ever good enough. The reason it is here has a name, and that name is Cpl. Jacob H. Turbett. For Jake. This was the last novel I wrote that he knew about. I had just finished the first draft by January 13, 2010, and I figured this would be a good place to start.

My little brother and I grew up always knowing where we wanted to be when we were adults. He wanted to be in the military and I wanted to be a published author. That little boy grew up to be a Marine, and was the only person who believed in me unconditionally. He would introduce me to his fellow Marines as "my sister, the writer." My dreams grew to include possible placement in the film industry, but never changed from the original "published author" bit, making a living by writing. Unfortunately, I dallied with college and a billion other things and he never saw my dreams come to fruition.

Jake was killed in action on February 13, 2010, during the first push into Marjeh, Afghanistan. He was 21 years old. I got a wake-up call, though for a while I was too distraught to see it. Now the first book of the Mermaid Chronicles, *Deep Blue*, becomes reality, hopefully with many more stories to follow. For Jake. I'd also like to thank Maria Vander Meulen, my amazing editor, and my friend Laura Klement for standing on the northern Oregon coastline in the middle of winter, in a bikini; just to get me a good cover for my book.

Thank you for believing in me. I will always believe in you.

Cpl. Jacob H. Turbett—My Hero

About the Author

Jaime E. Turbett currently resides in Portland, Oregon, with her two cats and her boyfriend. She loves to spend her days, reading, writing, adding to her movie collection, and playing cello with a local orchestra.